AVENGER'S TRAIL

AVENGER'S TRAIL

Lauran Paine

Sagebrush
Large Print Westerns

First published in Great Britain by Gresham
First published in the United States by ISIS Publishing Ltd

Published in Large Print 2005 by ISIS Publishing Ltd,
7 Centremead, Osney Mead, Oxford OX2 0ES,
by arrangement with
Golden West Literary Agency

British Library Cataloguing in Publication Data
Paine, Lauran
    Avenger's trail. – Large print ed. –
    (Sagebrush western series)
    1. Western stories
    2. Large type books
    I. Title
    813.5'4 [F]

ISBN 0–7531–7290–9 (hb)

Printed and bound by Antony Rowe, Chippenham

CHAPTER
ONE

For old Jubal the road had been long. There were times in a man's life when the spirit shrivelled from what lay ahead. Then anything carrying a man closer was pure torment. Usually though, what tired a man quicker than mountains and deserts, plains and prairies, was riding with indecision. For old Jubal Pierce there'd been this sensation of uncertainty right from the start.

It had happened back in Texas, in Deaf Smith County. Old Jubal and his two sons, Jefferson Davis Pierce and Robert E. Lee Pierce, came up from the plum thicket sink after four days hunting strays, hungry as she-wolves, tired and edgy, dirty and gritty-eyed. There'd been no one at the ranch to welcome them but one man, a neighbour named Forester. He'd taken them over to the town of Twelvetrees to see the bodies. Jubal's youngest daughter was first, all laid out in her blue party dress, while his eldest daughter, Maria, whose husband was along on the trail with the Pierces, was in the next pine box. They'd brought down one of Maria's gowns too, to lay her out in, and Frank Hudson, her husband, was sitting on his porch at their little ranch-home, rocking up and down, just rocking up and down.

They'd asked Maria if she'd like to stay with the youngest girl while her paw and brothers were down in the sink hunting cattle. That's how it happened Maria Hudson was there when the outlaws came.

Frank Hudson, though, wouldn't even look at old Jubal or the boys; he seemed to believe if Jubal hadn't asked Maria down to mind her sister while the menfolks were gone, his wife would still be alive. There's nothing anyone can say to a man who feels that way. Time, usually, time and common sense brings a distraught man to his senses, but they'd been on the trail now for five weeks — thirty-five days less one; the one day they lost following up a blind trail — and Frank Hudson still rode along with his eyes as dead in their sockets as though he and not his wife lay under the sod back there in Twelvetrees cemetery. He hadn't said a word. It was getting on the youngest boy's nerves. But then no one had ever truthfully claimed for young Bob Pierce a world of tolerance and patience. What young buckaroo has those virtues at nineteen?

For rawboned, hard-hitting, taciturn Jeff Pierce, twenty-six years old and who acted forty sometimes, Frank's bitter and silent anguish meant something else altogether. Jeff suffered it along with old Jubal. All the way up out of Texas where their trail led, over into New Mexico Territory where a nod here, an upraised arm there, kept them always seeking, always trying to make up those four days.

At first the trail was harder to find and keep to, but once out of Texas they gradually gained one day. Then two days. After that, however, the outlaws robbed a

2

stage near Deming and rode on the wind once more. What made it particularly difficult was that while the outlaws had funds, the Pierces and Frank Hudson had left Texas the hour after the funeral with exactly what lay between them — sixty-six dollars.

Another thing also made it hard for them. The out-laws stole fresh horses as they went along. Sixty-six dollars wouldn't buy but one good horse; old Jubal's jaw set like iron when yeasty Bob hinted they ought to do the same. He hadn't said anything, but then old Jubal didn't say much even when he was angry or indignant. But he could sure "look" a powerful lot.

So they kept riding their own animals, buying grain where they could, camping where the meadow grass and clover was rankest. Gratefully accepting a bait of hay in a cow-camp or at a ranch on their way.

One thing never deviated; their goal. Even when Jubal began having his doubts, his increasing uncertainty the farther they got from Deaf Smith County where folks understood things better, and it had nothing to do with the animals who'd slain their womenfolk; it had to do with exactly how they were going to exact their vengeance in some place like Arizona or California, or maybe even Oregon or Idaho, when they finally caught up, without being hanged themselves.

He mentioned this once to rawboned Jeff and got a cool look for his answer. "Paw; there's a heap of ways to skin a cat. I don't aim to get lynched by a band of range-riders or cow-town-men for doin' what's right, so

I aim to keep my eyes open, my mouth closed, and my horse shod all round."

Jubal Pierce was not a young man, but he rode and moved like one. The only concession he'd ever made to the weight of increasing years was to bed down a little earlier at night so that when he awakened between four and five every morning, he'd be able to roll out and grope for his gun, his hat and boots, without feeling tired and cheated — and old.

It wasn't much of a chore though; Jubal had worked hard all his life. He'd buried his woman when his four children were half grown. After that he'd simply worked harder in order to build up his herd, his ranch, and at the same time raise up his young 'uns fearing God, detesting liars and thieves, believing a man's word was his bond, and taught each of them to ride well, shoot straight, and always keep one eye on any trouble that might be in the making.

But the uncertainty nagged; by the time they'd left Deming behind with all the information they needed to reach the next town, the indecision was very strong. So strong in fact old Jubal was slyly figuring ways to slip away in the night, ride on ahead as fast as he could, catch up with their prey, and do what must be done without involving Jeff, Frank, or quick-tempered, fast-gun Bob. For a man'd who already buried a good woman, and now two daughters, it went sorely against the grain to also perhaps have to bury two sons and a son-in-law.

But Fate or some other dimly understood agent intervened. When they reached the village of Libertad

4

an old Mexican known as Juan The Watcher said to Jubal, "No, *Señor*, there were only five of them. I know that because I am crippled, *Señor*, and only sit now and watch who rides across the plaza, who are the strangers coming to Libertad — and when do these strangers ride away again."

Bob smiled and tossed old Juan The Watcher a half dollar. "Six rode in, five rode out. You boys hear that? Six rode into this place, but only five rode out again."

Jeff's gaze sharpened slightly towards Juan The Watcher but Frank Hudson seemed as before, expressionless and silent, even though he kept his eyes upon the old Mexican.

"Tell us, *viejo*, about that one who stayed," asked Bob. "He lives here; he perhaps has a wife here, or a sister."

"*Si*," agreed Juan The Watcher. "He lives here, *Señor*. He grew up here. His name is Joe Riley. But no; he has no sister or wife. He was a good cowboy at the ranches around Libertad, and they say when he's been drinking he is a devil."

Old Jubal led them on across the plaza to the public corral where they turned out their horses, bought them some feed, and stood back considering the town of Libertad. It wasn't much; another Mex town as old as the faraway hills, which had probably been old when Mexico ceded the entire southwestern United States to the Federal Union of North America.

It hadn't changed much since those days either except that the complexion of the ranchers grew lighter, modifications were inserted into the cow-working processes, English words superseded Spanish words, but otherwise there was still just the one broad central roadway, laid out straight and proud, while elsewhere beyond those two opposing ranks of storefronts, the citizenry had been at liberty to erect adobe houses wherever they wished to do so. This of course resulted in a tangle of paths and crooked little roads which, after nightfall for a stranger, could be a maddening maze.

Libertad was in fact a typical New Mexican town. Its economy dried up when the desert around it became incapable of supporting cattle and the big ranches drifted their herds northward towards better cow country each mid-summer. During winter and spring, though, Libertad would have its share of laughing cowboys, mostly Texans, with a scattering of northerners from Colorado, perhaps, or Nebraska. Then of course the stores, saloons, gaming rooms, would be lively. But this wasn't the lively time. Heat hung over the desert like a sickness nothing could dislodge or cure. It was a smoky haze during daylight and it was a sticky blanket that rolled up stiflingly at night. Libertad was silent, lethargic, seemingly abandoned.

Of course there were people; quite a number of them in fact who'd lived in Libertad for many generations and knew nothing different to this town and this environment; were inured to its heat, its totally unpredictable and unreasoning wintertime flashfloods, and its coming and going of strangers during the grazing season. Like crippled Juan The Watcher, all the people of Libertad saw things simply because they had very little else to interest them.

Old Jubal knew places like this; knew how the word would pass swiftly that four Texans had ridden in. Eventually, when the question was asked about where this Joe Riley could be found, that too would carry over the countryside in whispers, for these people knew avengers when they saw them, the same as people everywhere scented the odour of death when it arrived in their vicinity.

Jeff thoughtfully said, "What about the others? The longer we delay in this place the farther along they'll be getting."

Jubal had that answer. "Joe Riley'll know names and places. We won't have to track 'em no more after Libertad. We'll just go by other things."

Jeff was placated. Frank Hudson listened as he always did, and said not a word. Young Bob was softly restless. "Let's get on with it", he told his father. "Standin' around the public corral won't put us no closer to Riley. He'll be right here in this town somewhere. Probably with some girl."

"We'll eat," said Jubal, and led the way across the plaza towards a *tortilla* shop. They were the only people abroad, except of course for Juan The Watcher, who was in deep shade on across the plaza, his hat tipped down, his bent legs propped up, his very black eyes following their progress across from west to east.

Tortillas were plate-sized, limp pieces of dough which, when fried, rolled and filled with beans and pepper-sauce, became enchiladas, or something else with a different name depending upon what stuffing was inside them. When tortillas were made with ground flour instead of ground corn they tasted like limp dough. In Libertad there were very few corn patches, so the tortillas sold to strangers were made of flour, and except for their stuffing, wouldn't have appealed very strongly to anyone at all.

The man at the little café who waited on them was fat and short and sported an enormous Longhorn moustache of which he was very proud. He also had twinkling eyes and a broad, wide smile.

Yes of course he knew Joe Riley. Almost everyone in the Libertad vicinity knew Joe Riley. He'd grown up on this same desert. His parents were buried here. He'd ridden for the cow outfits and had, as a matter of fact, sat right there in this very café, many times, eating tortillas and licking from the pinch of salt always balanced upon the back of one's hand.

What of him? Well; he had a knife scar on his temple — some fight or other; who remembers all the fights when the rangeriders fill a town? — he was a very dangerous man when drinking. Otherwise, Joe Riley was like most other riders. He was tough and sometimes troublesome, but he had a deep laugh and a reckless way to him. There was only one outstanding thing: Joe Riley liked the ladies. Once, he'd almost gotten his throat cut for sneaking in to see a married *Señora* right here in Libertad when her husband was gone on a trail drive northward. The husband was a man named Turcio. Juan Turcio. He was a tall, light, very jealous man who was equally as good with knife, gun, fists. Fortunately for Joe Riley, he'd left town the spring before, a year back, a day before Juan Turcio returned to town and heard the gossip. Turcio had gone after Joe Riley, but had never found him.

Jubal was interested. "And now that Riley's back," he prompted their host. "What will Turcio do?"

"Well, *Señor*," smiled the portly caféman with a palms-up gesture which indicated the question was unnecessarily naïve, "He will of course kill him, if they meet."

Jubal paid for their tortillas and led their way back out into the heat and the hush. "We'll have to beat Mister Turcio to Riley," he said, "so I reckon we'd best split up; each man to go a different way to ask his questions. Then meet down at the public corral tonight."

They strolled off, leaving Jubal troubled that circumstances had done this to him; had thrown a victim so suddenly across their path. He walked uptown towards the local *cantina*, planning to be the one who'd find Joe Riley first.

Across the plaza in shadows, Juan The Watcher saw all this, and guessed its purpose.

CHAPTER
TWO

A *cantina* anywhere in the Southwest — Texas, New Mexico, Arizona — is a saloon, and saloons in cow-towns are the clearing houses for information. Any kind of information. For the price of a beer a rider can learn which ranches are hiring, which crews are making up a drive, which cowmen are slave-drivers and which are not. But bartenders, Mex or otherwise, are discreet men; they have to be. When Jubal, the obvious stranger to Libertad, got all the local gossip from the barman, who also happened to be a Texan and who owned the *cantina*, and dropped his inquiry about Joe Riley, his host's pale blue eyes became sardonic. After all, a professional saloonman ran into this identical situation many times; he knew exactly when the small talk stopped and the serious talk began. This time Jubal's answer was a lot less gratifying than it had been when he'd queried Juan The Watcher.

"There used to be a lot of Rileys hereabouts. In fact over at the cemetery there's got to be at least seven or eight of 'em. Of course some spelt their names different, but it always sounded the same, mister. Now this particular Riley you're lookin' for — where was he when you run into him, and what'd he do?"

10

Old Jubal drank his beer and nodded for a re-fill. As the barman went about getting it Jubal studied the man closely. In every man there's a key; find it, and he'll tell you whatever you want to know, even though doing so may endanger him. When the beer came back Jubal said, "Run off without payin' a debt."

It wasn't exactly a lie although it certainly wasn't the entire truth either, and its purpose was to delude, so it wasn't honest, but Jubal could rationalize the deception easily enough. Especially since he had to find Riley first, and also since he and the others had been so many weeks on this man's trail that they were saddle-sore and bone-weary. The ends, in other words, justified the means.

"That sounds about right," said the barman. "Joe went away owin' me three dollars on a bar bill."

"Did he pay it when he returned?"

"Yeah. He was in last night, late. He paid it with a five dollar gold piece." The barman's pale eyes were guardedly amused. "First piece of gold money we've had around Libertad since I can remember." He grinned. "But money's money, ain't it?"

Jubal falsely smiled back. "Sure is. An' it looks like maybe I caught up with Joe at just about the right time to get my payment. Where's he workin'?"

The barman didn't even hesitate. "He's not workin'. He's lyin' around. He came back kind of lean and rode-down-lookin'. Said he wouldn't be stayin' in town long either, but you can find him over at the boardinghouse. It's run by the town marshal's wife, Miz' Turcio."

Jubal digested that with surprise, then asked, "Where's Turcio?"

"Juan? Oh; he's down to Soda Springs buyin' horses. Won't be back for a week maybe." The barman dropped Jubal a knowing wink. "For a stranger you got the picture about right. Or else you know Joe pretty well. Him an' Turcio's wife had somethin' goin' before Joe rode out the last time. My guess is that if Joe don't cut 'er fine and hit the saddle soon, Juan Turcio'll return and then we'll have somethin' to break the damned monotony around here — a funeral."

Jubal paid and sauntered back out into the fierce orange-yellow sunshine. He could, by glancing from beneath his tugged-low hatbrim, see down across the wide, dusty plaza-area to the public corral. There was no one down there. He could also see that crippled old Mex who'd welcomed them to town, sitting far back under a wooden overhang southward, exactly as he'd been sitting when they'd first rode in. Jubal had lived a long time; he knew the kind of person Juan The Watcher was. The cripple would miss nothing; chances were, he wouldn't say anything either. He would remain absolutely neutral although a word from him could betray the Texans and send Joe Riley fleeing on a fast horse. To Juan The Watcher, who was a Mexican and therefore would have no love for Texans, it would be amusing and interesting to see these lean, burnt-brown men with their dusty clothing and their black-handled guns, hunt down Joe Riley, who wasn't a Mexican either.

12

Jubal made a cigarette and smoked it half through before sauntering off in the direction of the roominghouse. So far only a cripple and a pale-eyed barman knew strangers were seeking Joe Riley, but by nightfall everyone would know it. By then, however, if Jubal's calculations were correct, it wouldn't matter because Riley would be dead and the night would drop its darkness over the swift withdrawal of his killers.

So at least the orderly sequences work in men's minds.

Libertad, like all Southwestern villages, quietly retired to loaf away the scorching hours each day. Village activity was greatest in the cool morning and much later, in the cooling dusk. When old Jubal appeared at the *hacienda Turcio*, there was no one around. The doors were wide, to catch and hold any stray breeze, but the large old adobe house was as silent as a grave.

Jubal went out back to look for a horse. He found him. He even found the saddle with J.R. carved into the cantle roll. There had been saddlebags too, but it only showed where they'd been now by the rubbed places.

He returned to the house by the rear yard. There was no need for caution; Joe Riley didn't know he was being hunted, in all probability, and he wouldn't have known who Jubal or the other Texans were if he'd encountered them face to face. Being that kind of executioner was best.

Inside, there was a vast kitchen with a small fireplace in one corner, built in the shape of a bee-hive, and despite innumerable coats of whitewash, soot showed

13

through; evidently boarders ate in this huge, low-ceilinged room, because there was a long, massive oaken table with benches on both sides of it. In the centre were the South-western condiments. A glass jar of pale yellow peppers — *jalapenos* — hot as Dutch love and infinitely more permanent. Ground pepper, dried garlic, spoons in a drinking glass, and a snatch of polka-dot napkin beneath all this. Also, there was a quite handsome, black-eyed, rather tall woman sitting at that table, her thick mane of wavy black hair caught close behind her head and falling nearly to her waist. She caught movement from her lowered eyes and looked up swiftly with an expression of expectancy. At the sight of dirty, whiskery, leathery Jubal Pierce, the look vanished. She said, speaking Spanish, "What passes, mister?"

In the same language Jubal replied: "Mister Riley, missus. I am to await him here."

The woman smiled, perhaps at Jubal's rough Spanish, perhaps because he was *el viejo* — old one — and had no appeal except a fatherly one. She said, "Sit down, *Señor*," in flawless English. "Joe will be back soon."

Jubal dragged off his hat, stepped ahead making certain they were quite alone in the room, and sat. The handsome woman was looking at a limp and dog-eared magazine. She asked if Jubal would like some lemonade. It would, he knew, be made the Mexican way, without sweetening and bitter as original sin, so he politely declined. She then studied him with sharp interest asking if he'd come a long way. He shrugged,

14

saying long enough, but that any riding in this kind of weather was murderous. Then he smiled blandly and asked how Joe was.

The woman was both forthright and guarded. It seemed to Jubal she possessed one of those dual personalities, each portion of which knew what the other side was doing, and refused to be involved with it. She asked Jubal if he'd known Joe Riley long, to which Jubal truthfully said, "Long enough, Missus. Plenty long enough."

"And you know he has other women, eh *Señor?*"

The black eyes were utterly still, waiting Jubal's answer. In this woman was the sheathed violence of a puma, or the unleashed passions of the wildcat. Jubal sighed; he'd been womanless these many years, and now he was capable of admiring without feeling the slightest bit of urgency. "He's young, missus, an' women often like his kind of flash."

"I should kill him," Turcio's wife spat. "I should skewer him in the bed and roast his heart over coals."

Jubal smiled. "Whoa, missus; I didn't say he had other women. All I said was . . ." Jubal didn't finish. A man's spurs rang softly from out back as someone came towards the rear door. Jubal turned on the bench, his right hand out of sight of the handsome woman. She also turned to see who was approaching.

It was Jeff. He stopped in the doorway gazing at his father, ignoring the woman. "Well," he said, his voice flat and devoid of surprise. "I reckon we all end the same place, eh?"

15

"If we all get the same answers," replied his father. "Riley'll be along directly, according to the missus here. You might as well come in and sit." To the woman old Jubal said, "My eldest son, *Señora*." She ran a slow glance up and down rawboned, quiet-eyed Jefferson Davis Pierce. Evidently she liked what she saw for she smiled, showing perfect white teeth and soft dimples in each cheek.

"Joe has good looking friends," she murmured as Jeff removed his hat. "I'll get us all some lemonade."

Jeff's eyes lingered on the woman as she arose, padding away on sandalled feet. Her breasts were high, her shoulders straight, her back long and supple. He stayed over by the door saying nothing. When she brought him his glass he thanked her without showing anything in his eyes, the way an admiring man always does when he's impressed by the animalism of womenkind.

She took a glass over to Jubal and sat down across from them with the third glasss. Something died in her black eyes; something was in the atmosphere she could feel, now, and it turned her inward, turned her uneasy and anxious.

"Mister," she said in English to Jeff. "You rode with Joe Riley too?" She hung on Jeff's answer, but he was equal to it.

"Rode with him lots of places," lied Jeff Pierce, and sipped the mouth-puckering lemonade. Then he also did as his father had done, switched the subject. "This sure is good, *Señora*. Nothing like real Mexican lemons, eh?"

16

When the third dusty, gaunt, cold-eyed man appeared, Juan Turcio's wife became more anxious. The third arrival was silent, dull-eyed Frank Hudson. He neither removed his hat nor more than dropped one slatey glance upon the woman. He jerked his head at the other two and went back out into the rear yard. They at once followed him.

Bob was out there with their horses saddled and bridled. Yeasty young Bob saw the woman behind them and drank in her dark beauty even as he drawled to his older brother and father. "Let's go; there's been a little change in plans."

They didn't inquire. If they had they'd only have gotten another ambiguous answer, which they knew, so all three of them trooped on over, climbed across leather, turned and rode down the side of the house where the heat bounced back over them like hell's own fire, and followed the youngest among them down among the hovels and homes until the way was clear to depart from Libertad by the northerly routes.

Frank had nothing to say. Jeff was taciturn by nature, somewhat like his father. It was old Jubal, after they'd loped a mile across the shimmering desert, who hauled up and said, "Where you figure to take us, son?"

Bob turned his bronzed, thin features. "To Joe Riley, paw. Just tag along we're near the end of this trail."

"Whoa, son," called out old Jubal, holding his horse back. "How do you know where he is?"

Frank Hudson spoke. "He was with a girl in one of the shacks south of town. I was told that by a drunk. This drunk was the girl's father. I got Bob an' we waylaid him comin' out. Just follow Bob." Frank stopped speaking, set the spurs to his horse and loped around Jubal and Jeff to take position beside Bob. That's how the four of them rode the rest of the way out to where Bob and Frank Hudson had taken Joe Riley, with his arms bound at his back, and his ruddy, coarse face white to the eyes with thorough fear.

He was still tied to the tree when the four horsemen walked up on him. His shirt was wet through. Sweat ran from his forehead down into his pale, stricken eyes. While the four avengers sat motionless atop their horses, Joe Riley, who was about twenty years of age judging from his face, read their irrevocable purpose in each lean, dark set of features, and began to die an inch at a time.

Jubal swung stiffly down, went ahead and squatted Indian-like at the bootless feet of Joe Riley. "Give me five more names," he said quietly, his sunk-set old eyes as immutable as stone. "My boys have told you who we are and why we're here for you. A man never lives long who does things like that to women. Give us the names of the others, then get on your feet."

Bob untied the rope holding Riley to the base of the old, stunted tree. Overhead a bitter yellow sun burned down like fire. Gelatine waves of heat sluggishly undulated. Sweat dripped from the men as well as from the horses. Even the slightest movement was an effort. Riley carried a little spare weight while none of the Texans had even an ounce of fat, so Riley sweated harder.

"You can't shoot a man like this," said the captive, frantically seeking some hint of pity in those smoothed out, closed-down faces. "You can't just up an' murder a man."

"Five names, boy," purred old Jubal. "An' where they'll be. Make it quick, the day's fast slippin' away now."

Riley had nothing to trade with but he desperately tried. "I'll give 'em to you. Just set me free and leave me be."

Young Bob lifted out a two-edged Mex bootknife that coldly reflected the hot sunlight. "One ear," he told Riley, "then the other ear, then an eye, and the other eye. Give us those five names, Riley. *Now!*"

"Jeezuz," moaned Joe Riley. "Listen men; we didn't mean for 'em to die. We just rode onto the house an' they was alone an' . . ." Riley licked his lips. He was very close to fainting. "All right; Jack Slade from Lighthill, Pat Potter from Albuquerque, Mike Donlan from Taos, Lucifer Ames from Deming, and Joe Smith from Deming too."

Young Bob put up his bootknife and fell to working with the ropes on Riley. As he did this he said, "Joe; where were they going after they dropped you off at Libertad?"

Joe, hope surging as he watched young Bob freeing him, said in a rush of enormous relief, "To Spencer. It's sixty, seventy miles on west. To hit a bank over there. Now can I go?"

They stepped back and nodded. Joe Riley rubbed his bruised wrists, dripping sweat and looking into their

19

unrelenting faces. Then he broke and ran. They let him get several hundred feet and shot him to death. Then they mounted up and headed on west again with night close by.

CHAPTER
THREE

Most towns in New Mexico Territory had Spanish, or Mexican, names. When a town such as Spencer turned up it was a reasonably safe bet it had been founded by Yanquis. Usually, since there was little to draw men to New Mexico except mining and cattle, the towns had sprung to life under the impetus of one or the other.

But since Spencer lay across the broad deserts in a low, green valley with the Pajaro River close by, and there weren't any mountains closer than fifty miles, this time it had to be a cattle economy which made the wheels turn, the stores thrive, the people industrious.

Jubal led his sons and his son-in-law on the hard ride away from Libertad. Not that he expected pursuit, for even if they found dead Joe Riley back there in the dark, which was highly improbable, there hadn't been too many men back there who'd struck Jubal Pierce as the kind who's saddle up swiftly, form a posse and take after his killers. Even the town marshal, Juan Turcio — who probably wouldn't have tried very hard to find Riley's killers anyway — was out of town.

Still, that nagging sense of responsibility drove old Jubal hard. Until they'd toured half the night and Jeff called indignantly for a halt near a stone water-trough in a grassy little secret swale, Jubal hadn't even slowed his gait.

By then, according to Jeff's reckoning, they were a long fifteen or twenty miles from Libertad. "No one's goin' to wander out on that desert back there and find Riley before sunup, so there's no point in killing our horses," protested Jeff. "We'll off-saddle here and let the critters tank up and get a gutful of this greenery." Without awaiting word from his father, their nominal leader, or the others, big, rawboned Jeff stepped off and went to work hauling his rig down from the horse's back.

They had food with them in their saddlebags and the night was pleasant. It was also moonless so they had no chance to see exactly what might lie around them. Not that they worried after Frank Hudson made a long walk out and around, then came back to hunker with the others in deep silence while he also ate. If Frank'd found anything worthwhile he'd have spoken. Since he was silent, they relaxed.

Bob said, after they were finished eating and were lying back in the cool green grass, "They may scatter after they hit the bank in Spencer. They'll break up after one of these jobs. Their kind usually do."

Jeff had evidently been thinking somewhat along these same lines for he said, "It can't be much farther. If we light out about sunup, we're bound to see the place in time. Unless they hit the bank yesterday, they'll be figurin' on doin' it today. Maybe if we split up — two northward, two southward — we could head them off afterwards."

"Unless they go east or west," put in old Jubal, savouring the fragrance of his brown-paper cigarette. "Then we wouldn't have no better start on 'em than a posse'd have." Jubal sucked back a big, deep-down inhalation, let it slowly out and morosely said, "You got to remember, boys, and you got to remember well: from this night on we won't be the only hunters. We killed a man back there in cold blood. No matter how we look on it or the folks back in Deaf Smith County'd look on it — that was murder. Folks don't take kindly to murder, even when it happens to a man like Riley. You got to ride from now on with one eye raking every direction behind and southward, whilst the other one's raking forward and northward. If we get them others, the hunt'll be on for us strong, too. You better get used to livin' with that."

They didn't argue. They wouldn't have argued with what Jubal had said at any time. They'd known this would be the case sooner or later, but they'd all of them, even old Jubal, had thought they'd find the murderers and maulers of their womenfolk all together. That's what they'd been planning for: one furious gunfight. This was turning into something else quite different.

But the original thought didn't die easy. Young Bob said, "Those other five'll be in a bunch, when we find 'em, more'n likely. They'll have to stay together until they're plumb away, then they'll stay together until they split the loot. That'll give us time, I figure, to catch up with 'em."

Jubal sat moodily smoking, taking no further part in the conversation for a long while. The nagging uncertainty was now crystallized in his mind; he'd made his two sons, and Frank Hudson, murderers. There was another way of looking at it of course, but this far from Deaf Smith County, no lawman they might come onto was going to see it any way but as murder.

So it hadn't happened as he'd wanted it to. After all, a man crowding sixty doesn't have to be too careful of his life. There just can't be too many years left at that age, and if a man wants to toss them all into the pot on one gamble, one back-shot, then he can do it and to hell with the odds.

But young Bob over there lolling on his back softly speaking, smoking his cigarette — he was nineteen years of age. Jeff, who'd always been grave even as a small child, was twenty-six. That was young also.

Old Jubal got up and walked out a ways, over towards that ancient stone trough. There were stars above in a huge bowl of blue-black night. What had he done? Why, at his grizzled age, had he thought so much like a young man bent on vengeance? He didn't have a son-in-law any longer, or two boys of his own flesh, instead he had three cold-blooded murderers.

It would have been so simple, the old-fashioned way before folks got so strong on book-law. But that didn't help any; looking back never helped any, except in recollection of the soft, warm moments when a man was young and his woman was there.

That was all ashes now too. It was even getting difficult to recall her laugh, her smile, her tears. "God," he murmured, standing beside the stone trough, "I done it. I sure done it this time, God."

Back at their camp, with blankets unrolled upon the warm earth Jeff told the others it stood a little thinking on, what the old man had told them. He also said it'd take a little getting used to for men who'd minded the law all their lives to awaken in the morning as the worst kind of criminals — as murderers.

Bob wasn't so solemn about it. He said, "Jeff; that's what we been near six weeks on the trail to do. Why should it upset paw like this — and you? I been ridin' every day lookin' forward to the time I killed 'em, an' as for it bein' murder, I don't think that's it at all. I call it plain execution."

Frank Hudson, who'd listened for an hour to each of them, put a hat-shadowed stare upon the younger one, and nodded without opening his mouth. Since firing into the back of Joe Riley, Frank seemed to have come out of his shell a little. Now, with the weakest kind of starshine to help, Frank went about cleaning his sixgun, wiping out the barrel, wiping off each bullet as he replaced it in the cylinder, rubbing the firing pin free of all trail-dust and grit.

The old man returned as Jeff was making a fresh smoke. They glanced up then down again. In the blurry light of late night Jubal seemed a lot older than he'd seemed during hot daylight. He sat cross-legged, saw what Jeff was doing and started making another cigarette for himself. For moments they were silent and withdrawn from one another. Farther back the horses ate hungrily. They'd had precious little green grass since entering New Mexico Territory. They were tucked up and in need of the rest they would get this night.

Young Bob propped himself on one elbow gazing at his father. "You reckon we ought to light out of here now, paw?"

"I told you before — no. We need the rest. So do our animals."

"I'm fresh. So's my horse. Why don't I mosey on ahead and scout up the country around Spencer?"

"You stay, boy. You're young. All that means is that you don't tire easy; that you bounce right back. But it also means you're impatient, unsteady. We'll just sleep here for a few hours. Come sunup we'll head out again, all of us fresh and ready."

Frank Hudson spoke, wiping off his gun and gazing at it. "If we went into this here town one at a time it might be better. They'll have stages runnin' between Spencer an' Libertad. They'll hear about it bein' four mounted men who killed that Riley feller over in Spencer. It'd be better if we didn't show up all together."

They pondered that. Frank made a good point. Jubal, more interested that his son-in-law was emerging into their world of common awareness, nodded. He'd use Frank's idea. He said he thought they ought to bed down now, and set the example by lying back on his single old blanket, resting his head atop his battered old sweat-stained hat, and closing his eyes. He had no difficulty falling asleep. Ordinarily, he tried to be asleep much earlier. At his age it made arising in the pre-dawn morning a lot easier.

The others also bedded down. Both the older men didn't move again, once they got comfortable, but young Bob squirmed. He wasn't sleepy. He'd ridden as long, as hard as the others but he'd never shot a man before like that, and the vividness of everything a man does when he's only nineteen years old, appears to him sharp-limned, twice the size of life itself. He lay and recollected, imagined there was pursuit out somewhere beyond this camp of theirs in the menacing night. He pictured the other five they'd also kill. He could even imagine how they'd do it each time after this. The others wouldn't cringe and moan as Riley had done. They'd make a fight of it.

That thought quickened Bob's blood, tightened his guts into knots, made the night smell clear and sharp to him, made his vision clearer. He tossed on his blanket, almost believing everything that vivid imagination told him. His palms sweatted and he squirmed on his blanket.

He fell asleep only an hour or two before Jeff reached over and kicked the bottom of his foot, saying it was time to go.

There was a very thin bluish streamer outlining the raw-cut far horizon. The chill had increased right down to this last pre-dawn hour. The old man looked grey and cold as he stiffly went about shrugging into his jacket before going out to fetch back his horse where his outfit lay.

There was no dew on the grass, which they all noted. Dewless mornings meant sizzling hot days. But as they rode westerly again, leaving the stone trough behind and pressing ahead one more time across gravelly desert, the promise of heat to come was forgotten. Somewhere up ahead lay another town. This time they'd slip in like wolves, quietly and carefully, and eternally watchful.

Jeff and Bob broke their night-long fast with a smoke but Jubal was unconcerned. Frank cleared his pipes noisily and spat for a half mile after they'd left their campsite, then he caught hold of a cured grass stalk and munched on that.

They hadn't been in Libertad long enough to shave. Since they'd left Texas without spare clothing and only a couple of times had been able to bathe and wash out their attire, they looked a little harder each day thereafter until, as they rode now, their appearance was mean and sordid. Also, sweating themselves down as they'd done, riding straight on through regardless of the punishing heat, their faces were burnt nearly black and their eyes had the perpetual, wary squint of either the hunted or the hunters.

That's how they'd look to others. To one another they simply looked grimly dogged, unshaven and travel-stained, armed to the hilt and eager to find the end of their private avenger's trail.

Frank Hudson suddenly and softly raised his left arm pointing rigidly ahead. "Yonder," he muttered.

They saw the place rising up unevenly on the lifting slope of far-away desert, clearly defined in thin morning air with a weak little pinkish strand of dawn sun upon it. It didn't look like much of a town, only a little larger than Libertad in fact. Jubal rubbed his scratchy jaw.

"Seems hardly big enough to have a bank in it," he said.

They looked at one another as the same thought struck. Suppose that damned Joe Riley had lied to them after all; suppose Spencer didn't have a bank — which would mean of course the others wouldn't be up there planning to rob it.

"It better have a bank," snapped Bob.

Jeff and Frank rode silently gazing ahead, watching Spencer stand straight as they rode closer. The place sat upon a sort of gentle rise, or low plateau, with the desert all around it, but there'd been wells dug up there because the sight of green patches always meant water in this wasteland. The town, too, assumed several different shapes as the men got steadily closer until, only a couple of miles out, it began to show up as perhaps twice the size of Libertad instead of only half again as large. That reassured them all. Jubal said he'd probably been wrong. He sounded relieved about that.

"It's big enough to have a bank all right."

"It's quiet," observed rawboned, unsmiling Jeff. "Don't hardly seem there's been a holdup or the place would be showin' more life than it is, seems to me."

"One of two things," muttered Frank. "Either they held up the bank yesterday early and folks are over their first rash, or they haven't done it yet. One or the other."

This also seemed to make sense to them. Jubal poked along until he spied another of those stone watering troughs not quite a mile out, then angled for it. "We got to wash up," he said. "Bein' strangers'll make folks wonder enough without ridin' in dirty like we'd been on the trail all night. We got to handle things from now on real careful, f'like Frank said last night, there'll be a stage along directly from Libertad, and if they've found Riley back there the word'll spread right fast."

The trough was fed by a rusty old windmill, still now in the dawn hush. The water was as clear as glass and twice as cold. But it also stung them all wide awake. Afterwards, they beat off the trail dust, punched their hats into presentable shapes, allowed their animals a drink and a respite, then got astride again and walked onward, reins flopping, taking the measure of this next town.

Over the past weeks they'd ridden into, and out of, so many Libertads and Spencers they couldn't even recall all the names, and except for one thing, all the other towns had looked alike to them. This time, as mankillers, there was even a sharper scent to the air around a town; their glances were quicker and colder too. They were entering their first town as murderers, as men soon to be wanted by the law of New Mexico Territory.

Jubal reminded them again of this, stressing caution, then he told them they'd split up out here and each one enter the place from a different direction, and rendezvous at the nearest public corral an hour or such a matter from now.

CHAPTER
FOUR

The way the town of Spencer was situated put one in mind of the ancient Toltec civilization of pre-historic Mexico — except that nobody in New Mexico Territory knew there'd ever been such a thing as Toltec civilization. The only Indians they'd ever known hadn't had a civilization, unless a man called killing and plundering for a living was being civilized. Anyway, the town sat upon the highest bench of land in a broad, greeny oasis in the middle of an enormous expanse of desert cow-country. The sun struck the town first, always, because it was slightly higher than the rest of the surrounding country.

There were wells all around. In fact, a householder could dig his domestic well in one day because the nearby Pajaro River, sluggish and shrunken as it was this time of year, filtered underground for a considerable direction both to the west and east.

Spencer had a bank all right; it also had a modernized adobe jailhouse with real steel bars in the deep-set little windows. There was a general store with men's and lady's styles prominently displayed in a glassed-off front window; latest styles from places such as Denver, San Diego, and Tombstone. There were at least five saloons, harness and saddle shops, a stage office directly across from the *Pajaro Valley Hotel*, a one-storey, barracks-like rooming-house, two liverybarns and plenty of people coming and going. There was also the law. Town Marshal Ted Withers, who was also a special deputy U.S. marshal for the Pajaro district. As town marshal, Withers' jurisdiction was strictly limited to the town limits, but as a deputy U.S. marshal, he could go anywhere he wanted to go, not just in the county, but also over State lines if he had to.

This wasn't an un-heard of matter; frequently where no Frederal marshal's office was nearby and where a town lay upon some well-used outlaw-trail, such appointments were made by the nearest U.S. Marshal's office.

Ted Withers was a large man. Actually, he didn't stand over six feet tall, but he weighed right close to two hundred pounds, all bone and muscle, which gave him the appearance of considerable size. He was known as a tough, rough individual who'd face a buzz-saw. He'd come west to the Pajaro country six years earlier. Some said he was a Texan, but if that were so he didn't drawl like one.

Spencer had other local luminaries too, such as Roger Small, the banker, and Captain Sam Salton, proprietor of the large general store, who, it was said, possessed the largest bank account in all Pajaro County.

But like Libertad, a day-and-a-half's buggy ride eastward, Spencer had its doldrums when the desert cowmen drifted their herds north to greener country

32

each mid-summer. Still; there were plenty of people left. Enough left in fact so that an individual stranger attracted slight attention. There was one more reason why strangers weren't heeded too closely in Spencer when they came along individually: Spencer'd had no real trouble in four years. Fights among rangemen, yes, when the season was on, but no real trouble, therefore the place was placid and sweltering, relaxed and drowsy.

One thing was obvious; there'd been no bank robbery. Something else seemed rather obvious too; if there were five professional outlaws in Spencer, no one knew it, for the tenure of every-day existence coasted along through the stifling heat without a ripple of apprehension anywhere.

When Jubal and his sons met out back of town, westerly, where the only public corral stood, they exchanged impressions, each of them expressing this identical conviction. Jeff said that their biggest problem, since they didn't know the five men they wanted by sight, and since they certainly wouldn't be using their correct names right now, would be to identify them.

Frank had the pragmatic answer to that, as he often had to their similar difficulties. "We'll know 'em when they hit that bank. We just got to hang around here and wait."

That appeared as the best answer. Jubal concurred with it as they stood together like conspirators with the heavy layers of dusk dropping one by one over the empty land. Young Bob said, "Hell; if they didn't hit the bank yesterday nor today — maybe they won't hit it at all; they could've changed their plans. Maybe they aren't even around here. Maybe they're forty miles away by now."

Jeff shook his head. "I reckon they're around here," he said calmly. "If this is the end of their spree of robbin' and murderin', they'll want to end it with a big bang. Anyway; I don't think Joe Riley lied to us. He'd have no reason. Those names he gave us rang true. No Bob; I figure those men are close by somewhere."

"Where?" demanded the yeast youth.

The others paid no attention. Jubal remarked about the town marshal. Jeff and Frank had also seen him. He looked, they quietly agreed, able to whip a bear with a broomstick.

"But we got no fight with him," growled Bob, acting as though he believed the others were over-doing this business of being cautious.

Jubal put a cold glance upon his youngest. "Boy; since last night believe me, we got a fight with every lawman we see. Even if it's only a fight to shy clear of 'em. You remember that. An' you remember somethin' else too. I'll say when we move, how and where. You just hold off and wait for the rest of us."

Bob subsided, sulking. He stepped past to lean upon the corral stringers looking in. Their horses had the whole huge corral to themselves. They'd purchased a bait of hay from the liveryman nearest this corral. The horses were wearily eating now.

Bob turned slowly, his disapproval of the caution of those older men suddenly gone. "Hey; it just come to

34

me. This here's the only public corral, that liveryman said."

"What of it?" asked Jeff, looking past his father's shoulder at his brother.

"Well; those five either got to use the public corral like we done, or stable their animals at one of the liverybarns — or else they stabled 'em privately, which'd mean they got friends here."

This thought was worth mulling over. For a while the older men gazed at Bob and stood silent. Frank Hudson finally said, "You overlooked something, Bob. None of them is from this town. It's possible they'd have friends here, but it's more possible they wouldn't contact 'em, if they aimed to rob this bank, otherwise their friends'd identify 'em afterwards."

"Then where the hell are their horses, Frank? You don't hide five horses that easy."

"They got a camp, boy," answered Hudson a trifle sharply, as though exasperated at the younger man's impatience. "They got a camp somewhere out a ways."

Again, Frank had made a good point.

Jubal said thoughtfully, "Could we find that camp before they break in an' head in here to hit that bank?"

Frank lifted his shoulders and dropped them. "Our horses've had just about all the hard use they can stand, Jubal. If them fellers raid the town tomorrow an' we used our horses hard tonight, we couldn't give em' much of a chase tomorrow, could we?"

"Too late to go huntin' 'em now anyway," put in Jeff. "We might as well bed down out here near our saddles and get at least one good night's rest."

Jubal agreed with that. He'd rather hoped — without much faith that it would happen — that one of them might pick up a scent while ambling about the town, but none of them had, and Jubal himself had been more concerned with hanging around the stage station to see if he could pick up a hint that Joe Riley's murder had been discovered over at Libertad. Apparently it hadn't, because none of the stage company men had any fresh gossip to pass around.

But Jubal didn't delude himself either; maybe no one would find Riley's carcass right away, but they'd eventually find it. In hot weather as hot as this meat spoilt fast; the gathering buzzards circling in their lazy spirals so near to Libertad would draw some curious soul. The most they could hope for, Jubal thought, would be perhaps one more day. At the very most, two more days.

He told the others his conclusions. "Whatever happens has got to happen tomorrow, boys. So far I figure we're clear over that Riley killin'. At least I detected no excitement around here today an' surely folks'd been gossipin' if they'd heard of it. So what it boils down to is a matter of time. Those men've got to hit that damned bank tomorrow, and we've got to be out of this country by tomorrow night at the soonest, day after tomorrow at the latest. By then we'll be the hunted ones, not those five we're huntin', if they don't hit the bank, and if someone finds Riley's body over at Libertad."

Jeff nodded, following all this reasoning clearly. "After nearly two months of riding," he murmured, "we've got to bring things to a head in one day. Time catches up with folks, I reckon."

They got their blankets, walked around to the far side of the public corral away from the gate so as to be out of sight if others came in the night to turn in their animals, and bedded down. They'd all had a decent meal this day — their first decent meal in a long time — and they were shaved now too, which gave them a fresh perspective.

"I think they'll hit the bank tomorrow," said Frank Hudson, prefacing this statement with nothing and adding nothing to it either, except one more curt sentence. "We got to know which way they'll go afterwards."

Jubal, loosening the rolled blanket from behind his cantle, said, "It's a riddle, Frank. Odds are against us guessin' the right direction. About all I can see for us to do is keep our animals saddled out back of town close to the bank so's we can light out the second we know the robbery's taken place."

That made sense. Bob agreed with it as he lay back upon his pallet. Jeff said nothing. He kicked off his boots, carefully placed his rolled gun-belt within inches of his hat, which would be his pillow, and sat cross-legged atop his blanket making a cigarette. The night around them had a sweet, curing smell as though the people who cut hay to sell to the liverymen and others, had fresh-cut their crop and perhaps had shocked it to dry.

Jeff lit up, gazing sombrely ahead through the warm night. It seemed to him their weakest link was the horses. They'd done their best for the animals since leaving Deaf Smith County, but with so little money amongst them they hadn't often bought grain. No horse, no matter how tough and durable he is, can keep going forever on washy green grass, and stronger, better roughage hay. Even grain won't more than put off for a while longer, the inevitable. Horses, like men, are made of flesh and bone.

"They'll have fresh animals again," he eventually softly said, not bothering to look around at the others who were stretched out atop their pallets. "They maybe spent today rounding them up. Our critters aren't very far from abandonin' us. We'd only be foolin' ourselves to think different, too."

"All we got to do is keep them men in sight," argued young Bob. "In fact; we could leave the posse that'll take after them do that for us, and take our time until the townsmen turn back."

"*If* they turn back," muttered Frank drowsily. "That town marshal's no greenhorn. He's a desert-man if I ever saw one. Those whelps aren't goin' to just run away from him. And Jeff's dead right. If we push the horses tomorrow, we'll wind up on foot."

"You talk like you're sure it'll happen tomorrow," muttered Bob, piqued that he'd been talked down so logically. "Remember, Frank, they've had a two-day lead on us for three weeks now."

Hudson lay perfectly still looking up at the stars. He didn't bother to argue. He wasn't an argumentative man anyway.

"It's just a feeling," said old Jubal. "They'll hit the bank tomorrow. The big question to me, is *when* they'll hit it. If it's about sunup or a little before, about like I reckon I'd want to do it was I in their boots so's I'd have coolness to run through afterwards, why then we can be over there waiting. But if it's tomorrow evening when everyone's at supper an' they'll be countin' on the night to shield them from pursuit, why then that'll be another story because it'll make it twice as hard for us too."

Jeff smoked and listened and sat cross-legged in his stockinged-feet saying nothing, his broad-shouldered silhouette a black outline against the paler gloom.

Their horses had finished the hay and were sipping water at the plank trough. It was customary to fill an empty Bull Durham sack with asafoetida and toss it into the watering troughs of public corrals in the belief that this disinfected the water, otherwise horses picked up everything from glanders to distemper from all using the same trough. Jeff could smell the asafoetida; it had a rank stench second to nothing in the realm of offensive odours.

He eventually killed his smoke and lay back, but lightly, not flat out like his companions; he didn't propose to sleep this night. What his father had just said in his drowsy slackening mood, had set Jeff to speculating.

He deduced that if a man were over there near the bank before sunup he'd be able to spy on anyone who came slipping silently towards the building. That would give them the answer they needed. If it turned out that no one came, Jeff could simply come back to his blanket, make an excuse for not arising in the morning, and make up the lost sleep during the day and be ready to try the same trick again along towards evening.

The more he turned it all over in his mind the better he liked his idea. He lay still, listening to the breathing of the others for a long while. Jubal dropped off first. Frank was next. It took young Bob a full hour to drop off, then Jeff silently eased up, took his boots and walked away in his stocking-feet as far as the corral. There, he dusted off his socks, donned the boots and stepped around the corral through weak moonlight to where he could see the few scattered night lights of town.

The place was as still and empty-seeming as a graveyard. He warily went along, buckling on his gun-belt as he moved, and eventually passed through back-lots and alleys until he was in the total darkness of an intersecting roadway. There, he chose his site for the long vigil ahead, and composed himself. It wasn't even midnight yet.

CHAPTER
FIVE

They came.

It wasn't sunup by a good two hours when Jeff saw the first man pass quietly on foot out back of the bank. He caught that one's movement between two buildings where moonlight reflected off glass windows. The man was on foot; he was carrying something under his left arm, his right arm swung free.

The second one wasn't so easily seen for an excellent reason. That one didn't walk down from the north end of town as had the first one; he instead came up from the south, and Jeff wouldn't have spotted him at all if he hadn't eased out onto the plankwalk southward, on across the road, to look both ways very intently. This second man was their sentinel, apparently, because after he'd reassured himself there was no one around, he stepped back into shadows beside a building, standing watchfully as Jeff was also standing, and made no additional move towards the rear of the bank.

Two more filtered down from the north end of town. Jeff guessed their strategy; they'd ridden in from wherever they'd been hiding on the desert, had dropped off the sentinel at the south end of town, then had completed their circle northward where the other three had brought their tools and had approached the bank building.

That left just one outlaw beyond town somewhere, perhaps northward, or just as possible eastward which would be closer when the robbery was completed and the men could rush straight out for their horses. He'd be sitting a saddle out there holding all their animals. He'd also be another sentinel.

For five more minutes Jeff stood like stone, listening and watching. He was sure each conjecture he'd just made was correct, but he wanted to be still more certain, so he stood up there around the first corner where the main roadway was intersected by this little side-road where he waited, and kept a close, almost breathless watch on the bank's one large front window.

The five minutes was nearly up when he saw, just for a fleeting second, the flicker of yellow light through that front window. That was all he'd wanted to see. Without waiting a moment longer he whirled, stepped off the plankwalk — which would hollowly echo his running footfalls — and hastened back around through town heading back for the public corral.

An old dog who wasn't asleep looked up when he trotted past some trash tins, barked once, then dropped his head and resumed his search for scraps of food or bones.

Jeff made no effort at keeping his approach secret as he ran towards the public coral, therefore, when he came around it on the far side, Frank and young Bob were sitting up, covering his shadow with their guns.

"Get up," he said sharply. "They're inside the bank right now!" As the other two gaped, he stepped over and shook his father awake. "They're robbing the bank," he reiterated.

Jubal unwound up off his blanket as though he were thirty years younger, took a step, cursed and turned back for his boots. Frank and Bob groped for their boots too. Jeff went across to the far side of the public corral and flung down the bars to step inside and catch his horse.

He was half-saddled before his father appeared, wet-eyed and grey around the lips with weariness, but firmly and grimly resolved. The last one to catch a horse was Frank. By then Jeff was already rigged out. He led his animal past the downed bars outside, tested his cincha out of pure habit, then swung up. The horses acted fresh and rested, which was good.

It took them ten more minutes. Old Jubal was beside his horse, Bob was bitting his beast and Frank was settling over leather when the explosion came. It sounded like a simultaneous barrage by steel cannon. The earth reverberated, breaking glass tinkled throughout town, and roiled air swept first one way then another way.

Jubal swore, jumped a foot, then grabbed for the stirrup and rose lithely up to settle over his saddle. "Get aboard," he barked at his youngest son. "Jeff; which way?"

Jubal meant which way would the outlaws go, but Jeff had no answer to that now, any more than he'd been able to guess the direction the night before. He booted out his horse and waved for the others to follow. The only thing Jeff did know right then was how to wend his way through the back-lots and alleys to the centre of town.

Bob caught up with Frank. They swept along behind Jeff passing houses where lanterns were just beginning to sputter to life. Now there were more dogs; the first shock of surprise had passed and Spencer was coming awake. The last echo of that blast had died and excepting the barking canines, the roll of riders passing hastily around towards the centre of town from the west, out where the public corral lay, there was the same late-night quiet again.

Jeff didn't head straight for the main thoroughfare. He instead dashed across it into the yonder back alley over behind the bank. Jubal was right behind him with Frank and Bob closing fast. They all heard the excited curses farther out where other riders were urging their horses easterly. That was all any of them needed.

The moon was so low now it didn't help the pursuers one little bit. In fact it hindered them by adding to the peculiarities of the dying night. They rode entirely by sound with big Jeff well ahead, straining to see what was hidden from them all — the outlaws getting away with their loot from the ravished bank of Spencer.

Distantly they heard a gunshot, then an answering shot, and finally a flurry of more shots back in town. There was no time to speculate about that right then, for out of the onward darkness a horse loomed up, acting bewildered and unsure which way to go. Jubal cried out at sight of the animal. Frank and Bob raced up beside the older man, guns ready. But the horse was riderless.

Jeff shouted to them as they swept past this beast. "One of 'em didn't get away. That'd be what the shooting was about back there. One of 'em got caught in town."

They heard this without acknowledging that they had. It was obvious to them now anyway, otherwise there wouldn't have been a riderless horse out here.

The night was cool. In fact this was the coolest time; an hour from now the sun would pop up off in the ancient east and after that, although they'd have adequate light to see by, they'd also begin to feel the buildup of summertime heat, which meant they wouldn't be able to push their horses so hard.

Jeff's idea, very clearly, was to overtake the outlaws before that happened, but what he'd remarked about the night before shortly became apparent. Their horses, fresh-fed and rested though they were, couldn't hold the murderous pace being set by the renegades, sunlight or no sunlight. They ran as gallantly as horses ever could, but after that first wild hour, they began to hang a little in their bits, to scuff dust for lack of lifting their feet high enough, and to mechanically rise and fall, rise and fall, without gaining an inch.

Jeff swore loudly as he heard the fleeing men drawing steadily away. His father rode grim-faced and tight-lipped, grey and sleepless and bleak to look upon. Frank snarled at young Bob for mercilessly rowelling his tiring horse.

"Go ahead and kill him, you fool, then you'll be afoot and that'll hold us all back!"

Jubal turned on his youngest with a black look. Bob pointed ahead with his right hand where that diminishing sound lay. "They're goin' to get clean away, paw."

"Ease off on that horse," roared the old man, angry all the way through. "We'll get 'em. We got this close an' we'll get this close again, but not with a dead horse amongst us. Now you ease off!"

They all eased off. Jeff looped his reins and spat at the dark earth with frustration. He then wiped clammy sweat off his forehead, re-set his hat and let the horse pretty much pick his own gait. They'd been out-run. Not out-thought, just out-run. So now the steady tracking would start all over again. But one thing was dead-certain: they were going to have to get fresh animals if they were to close that distance again.

When the sun peeped across the rim of the curving world, they were still riding at a little jog. It was faster than a walk and it was easier on their horses. Far ahead they could see dust. Far back too, they could make out other dust. They were between two armed and dangerous parties of horsemen, the hunted and the hunters.

"If you'd come the first second you seen 'em," railed young Bob at his elder brother.

"I had to be sure, boy," replied the rawboned, sundarkened older man. "I had to let them get inside that damned bank to be sure they weren't just some drunks staggerin' on home after the saloons closed."

"And these lousy horses," swore the upset youth. "Paw; I *told* you a long way back, we should've stolen fresh animals."

"We're not thieves," growled Jubal, narrowly watching the route of that forward dust-banner. "We'll get fresh animals first chance we get, but until then we'll keep on their trail."

That's exactly what the four of them did; they didn't stop until they passed the stone trough where they'd bedded down the night before they'd entered the town of Spencer. Then they only paused long enough to tank up the animals and pushed straight onward again.

The outlaws bent around, finally, heading southward. They also slowed their gait to conserve horseflesh too. Because the men from Deaf Smith County were making no dust, and also because they were out of sight, the renegades had no idea there was any pursuit closer than back many miles where the agitated possemen from Spencer were still punishing their mounts hard in an effort to catch up. This was in the favour of the Pierces and Frank Hudson. Jubal narrowly concluded it would make all the difference when the inevitable show-down arrived. But then old Jubal had been on manhunts before; he could correctly assess the odds, the options, the inevitabilities. His biggest problem right at that moment, as they kept the fugitives in sight, was one he wasn't entirely unaware of, but it didn't right then loom very large: Bob, his youngest, and that fiery, explosive temperament of his.

It was close to ten o'clock before Jeff made a cigarette for breakfast and scowled over the dark brown taste it imparted. By then the sun was well up, too, which meant the heat was dancing all around them once more.

Additionally, they didn't know the southward country over which they were riding. Frank Hudson said he hoped the outlaws knew it, otherwise they were going to be riding dry horses within another couple of hours.

There were no ranches, or if there were any down in this burnt out country, they were out of sight. From time to time they saw cattle and distinguished brands, but both were alien so they paid them scant attention.

The tracks their prey left upon the dusty desert were sufficient to keep the Texans heading right. It seemed that the outlaws were heading straight for Mexico, but that would be a long ride; they were confident there'd be towns long before any of them got that far southward. As Jubal pointed out, that river from up around Spencer had to wind down through here somewhere, and in New Mexico — as in Texas and most other places — where there was water, there were ranches, people, settlements.

At noon their horses were suffering from the blazing heat more than the riders were. Frank Hudson began growing gloomy over the immediate future. Young Bob, sullen since his father had tongue-lashed him for abusing his tiring animal, redeemed himself by drifting off a half mile eastward and finding a solitary cottonwood tree. From there, he rode down-country a short distance and found one of those stone troughs the desert cowmen laboriously built in preference to metal or wooden troughs, because stone and mortar didn't rot nor turn porous and permit the precious liquid to escape. He went back and led the others on over.

They killed a half hour in this place and were loath to leave it even then, although they knew their fugitives were still travelling. Old Jubal set the example by soaking the inside of his hat, his shirt, and by finally knotting a water-logged handkerchief around his throat. From that spot for the next four miles, until evaporation robbed them of all that wonderful coolness, they rode in relative comfort.

They also ate — four cans of oily sardines Frank had in his saddlebags — and turned down some salted jerky Jeff had in his saddlebags. The mid-summer New Mexican desert was no place to eat anything that was cured in salt.

Then Jeff discovered why the outlaws hadn't sashayed a little and refreshed themselves and their horses at the stone trough; there was another one five miles below and to the east a short distance. This one was larger, circular, and stood in the perpetual shade of a grove of cottonwood trees. Here, by the sign they left in abundance, the Texans figured out that the outlaws'd had a food cache here. They'd eaten well. They'd even had a half bag of barley for their animals.

"Not too far ahead now," opined Bob, standing in sweltering shade gazing down across the shimmering desert southward. "We'll maybe overtake 'em in the night."

Jeff snorted. "How? You figure they'll make a fire?"

Bob flushed and went sullen again. Old Jubal watched his horse nuzzle the empty barley sack and shook his head. "We'd better come onto a ranch or a cow-camp directly," he said. "The horses can't hold out more'n another day or so in heat like this.

Frank nodded without comment. He'd been making this point over and over again, but then it had been no secret for a long time now.

They left the circular trough with the sun sliding down the westward sky and hazing over with a pale pink dullness to it. Afternoon was well advanced but all that meant to the riders was more heat, more discomfort, more punishment for their trail worn animals.

But they kept at it. Now, however, since the outlaws were also travelling slowly, there was no dust-banner. They didn't need it, not with the tracks they had to travel by, but it could have helped if the renegades ever changed course enough to permit the Texans to short-cut them. That didn't happen. Jubal, who was accustomed to hardship, didn't expect it to happen either.

CHAPTER
SIX

The sun didn't set until eight o'clock. They'd been in the saddle since about five in the morning. That made a long day even under pleasant conditions. They hadn't had anything worthwhile to eat, less to drink, no rest, and had been brutally worked over by the blazing sun for all those hours. Even young Bob was wilting by the time the sun set.

But daylight still lingered, hot and glazed and still as death. The sun had been completely gone for an hour and there was no lessening of the light, only a lessening of the heat-hazed glare that bounced up off the tantawny desert to hit their faces.

Still; that was something in their favour, meagre though it was. Later, when the shadows began thickening all round, it remained just as bitterly hot as ever. In fact, it often got several degrees hotter after sunset for some strange reason. Jubal said it was because all the heat stored by earth and rocks and sandy places was released the minute the sun set; rose up like invisible smoke to start the cooling process, which worked from the ground up.

They didn't dispute him. They didn't know why it got hotter, they only knew that it did, and they were too near the edge of total exhaustion to even care. They were riding like automatons, rocking with each step of their animals out of sheerest instinct.

"They'll stop directly now," said Frank Hudson, when the shadows were puddling everywhere. "They'll put out a man to scout the back-trail a ways, and if he doesn't alarm 'em, they'll settle in for a spell."

"Maybe they'll divvy up the loot," croaked Bob through dry, cracking lips. "If we could come onto 'em doin' that . . ." Bob smiled murderously without ever completing his sentence.

"We got to stop directly too," muttered Jubal, who looked drunk and acted half-drunk the way he reeled now and then in his saddle. "I hope to gawd there's another of them troughs down here somewhere."

Frank had the answer to that. "You can bet your boots there is, Jubal. An' you also bet your boots there's where them devils is settlin' in for the night. If we just knew where the trough was."

They didn't know, and that was the point to work from. As Jess said, "We got to find it, Frank, but we can't do it on horseback. As soon as it's dark enough, you an' I better scout ahead on foot."

They rode until the night fell, softly and heavily, cooler after a while and therefore sufferable, and oddly enough when they halted it was the youngest who almost fell from his saddle as it was also the oldest whose mind was razor-clear in speculations.

"Scout parallel," said old Jubal. "An' not too far apart. If one of you stumbles onto somethin', the other one'll be close by to help."

It was the oldest and simplest method of scouting; it was also the practice among both soldiers at war — which old Jubal had once been in his lifetime — and hunters after redskins — which Jubal had also been.

He stayed back with the youngest and told the boy something that would have helped any inexperienced youth except that was precisely why youth was always inexperienced — because it was too young to take heed.

"Son; a man wears himself faster just thinkin' hard thoughts and bein' impatient. You set down over there after you loosen the cincha on your horse, and figure one thing to be sure as death: we'll get them. If not today, then tonight, if not tonight, why then tomorrow. That's all you got to concentrate on to make it happen, an' all the frettin' and stewin' in the world won't make it come any faster than it's supposed to come."

Bob cared for his horse and watched old Jubal care for the other three animals. Then he made a cigarette and smoked it even though his mouth was dry as chalk. Afterwards, with the heat lifting as though it were a lead weight over his bowed shoulders, he dropped flat back on the earth and closed his eyes. He was tormented by dehydration the same as were the others, but exhaustion made that other feeling seem less important right at the moment.

The night grew in weight and size and dark volume, until the thin moon appeared, and the stars. By then it was almost pleasantly cool, which helped. Jubal hunkered, smoking and listening. In the stillness of a summertime night on the empty desert a man could hear a leaf fall or a cricket rub its legs together. Louder noises, from farther off, were borne in as though they couldn't be more than a yard or two away.

It was inconceivable that anyone could stealthily approach, but they did. The way it happened had one weak excuse; Jeff and Frank returned just short of midnight, to drop down and say in quiet tones they hadn't found the fugitives. Jubal scowled; it wasn't possible they'd kept riding after dark when they had no reason to believe pursuit was close.

"Maybe they heard us back here," said Jeff, dispiritedly. "Maybe they had fresh animals staked out down here somewhere. But they sure as hell aren't anywhere around this place."

It was this demoralized conversation among them that permitted it to happen, but right up until a hoarse, unfamiliar voice spoke across the darkness to them, not a one of them believed it possible.

"Don't you fellers so much as move an eyelash!"

They obeyed. Not because they'd been told to but because they were too thoroughly astonished to do anything at all for several seconds.

"Now stand up, the four of you," commanded the same dry-tired voice, dragging off each word as though exhaustion made speech difficult even now in this critical moment of peril.

They arose, even young Bob, peering around and seeing nothing. Their gun hands held well clear of any weapons. What in the hell did the outlaws want with them? If it was their horses, that was going to turn into a very bitter disappointment.

54

One man moved forward out of the eastward darkness until they could see him well, and that stunned them all over again. It was the heavy-shouldered, hard-faced town marshal from Spencer, not one of the outlaws! He said, speaking from the corner of his mouth to someone back there in the night with him, "Go on up and take their guns. Now don't get between me'n them. Go around from behind. The rest of you kneel and take good aim. If one of them so much as wiggles — kill him!"

Jubal swallowed painfully. They'd been so intent upon the renegades on ahead, they'd made a terrible mistake; they'd entirely overlooked that posse of townsmen coming on behind them.

"Marshal," said old Jubal, "We're not the men you're after. They're still on ahead somewhere, southward."

"Is that a fact," croaked the lawman, "An' how would you know who we're after, oldtimer, if you didn't know what they'd done and why they run?"

Jubal's lips parted, but he didn't answer. How could he explain without saying too much? "Marshal; I give you my word we're not the ones. You can leave us right here under guard and head on down-country. You'll find them other ones if you ride hard."

The lawman studied old Jubal with a contemptuous glare, and said what was in the mind of every posseman who now walked forth into full sight, guns ready and cocked to kill. "Oldtimer; there were five of you back there inside our bank. We killed the one who didn't get out after the blast. That left four." The lawman raised a big finger. "One, two, three, four."

Jeff looked stiffly at his father, at Bob and at Frank Hudson, then he let all his breath out in an audible sigh. "Something sure as hell went wrong this time," he told them.

"Fate," said Frank. "Damned lousy Fate. This makes the second time lately it's turned on me. The first time was when it took Maria. Then this time."

The possemen got their guns and closed up in a ring of deadly, moonlighted faces. They were set to kill the men from Deaf Smith County.

Jubal said, "Marshal; if we was the ones we'd have the bank loot with us. Go ahead and search."

"You'll lead us to it," growled Ted Withers. "This young one here, oldtimer, is he your son?"

"My youngest. This big one is my oldest."

"Damn your rotten soul; what kind of a father makes thieves out of his children? You're lucky I'm bound by oath, otherwise I'd see you hanged, all four of you. Now; where did you cache the money?"

Jubal shook his head. "Marshal; we are not the ones and that's Gospel truth."

Several townsmen growled low and menacing as they moved in closer. The lawman looked down his hawkish nose at them but said nothing. A lanky man who was hatless put up his sixgun and stood close enough to see all four prisoners. He said nothing; he was the only one, it seemed, who didn't have something to say.

Marshal Withers bitterly reflected and eventually put up his gun too. "Oldtimer," he exclaimed, "you're temptin' Fate right now. These men — some of 'em —

had money in that bank. I'm only one man if they decide you fellers need hanging."

Frank Hudson, who hadn't said a word up to now, looked with patent scorn upon the big man. "It'll be on your conscience, and if we're not the ones you'll find it out sooner or later. All of you. Then tryin' sleepin' well at night. What the hell makes you think the men who robbed your bank are the only ones riding this country?"

The man who'd stood back making a silent judgment with both arms crossed upon his chest, said, "I got doubts about this, Ted," to the angry-faced lawman. He didn't raise his voice nor speak loudly. "Let's have no more talk before we do something we'll be sorry for. Just put 'em on their horses and take 'em back."

The others stopped their growling. Even the marshal listened to this lanky, hatless man with the grey above his ears and the very steady, steely eyes set in a youthful-looking face.

One man spoke up; he was short and wispy and sinewy; one of those rattlesnake-quick, deadly men. "Cap; it's got to be them. Hell's bells; there's four of 'em an' they knew the bank'd been robbed even before we tol' 'em. An' look at them horses: rode down to a shadow. They're strangers to boot."

The hatless man quietly conceded these points. "I'm not saying this isn't the gang. I'm saying we'll take them back to Spencer and try them." He looked down into the upturned, malevolent eyes of the wiry man. "If they're the ones, we'll find out where they cached the money. Now let's head back while the night's coolness is still around." He slowly turned and locked glances with Marshal Ted Withers.

Jubal spoke up. "Mister; I realize now how it looks to these men, and probably to you also. An' I appreciate that you're a law-abidin' man. But do us all one favour. Detach a man or two to scour this desert on southward. I pass you my word the men who hit that bank are down there. Me'n my boys'll go back with you without any trouble. Just put a man or two to scoutin' the south country."

The man called Captain was solemnly studying old Jubal through this plea, and finally he nodded. The others made groans of disgust; they didn't believe a thing Jubal had said and were perturbed that the hatless, lanky man did believe. He turned on them, eyes flashing, and gave his reason for acting as he now acted.

"What's the matter with you men? You saw the tracks, dammit all. You've been following them all day. One set of four imposed over another set of four."

Marshal Withers gave his head a disgusted shake. "Cap; you know what we decided. They were leadin' extra horses."

"Then where are those extra horses?" demanded the lanky man, his voice turning impatient with his companions. "Where did they set the other animals loose? Ted, you know damned well we watched for sign of them being turned loose and didn't find it."

Marshal Withers screwed up his face. "You mean you *believe* these men, Cap?"

"I mean if we stand around here talking ourselves into a lynchin', Marshal, that'll be as bad as having our bank robbed." For a moment the lanky, hatless man looked around at his companions, scorning them with his commanding gaze. Finally, locking glances with Marshal Withers once more he said, "There's a law against lynch-parties too, and I will not be party to anything like that. And in case you've forgotten — I lost more money in that robbery than anyone else."

Ted Withers shifted his stance. This exchange seemed to embarrass him a little. In the end he looked darkly around. "Get the horses," he growled at the possemen. "Cap's right about one thing anyway; we got 'em, and by gawd they'll tell us where they cached that money, so I reckon we'd better head on back."

The hatless man said, "John; Carl; ride on down-country. When dawn comes see if there are another set of tracks leading away from this place. Don't try to make a contact if there are, just high-tail it back to town and let us know. It shouldn't take long for you to make out whether these men have lied to us or not."

Two rough-looking men nodded and drew off apart from the other possemen, their faces grave and uncertain as though they weren't sure what to believe.

Jubal said, "Mister; we thank you. And I didn't lie."

The man called Captain looked with coldness on old Jubal. "I think maybe that you did lie, oldtimer, but if you didn't, and there are others down here — another party of four who could've robbed our bank — we'll get them too."

"How?" asked young Bob. "Mister; my paw told you the truth, but if you turn back now you'll never get 'em. They'll have a full day's lead."

The hatless, greying man said, "Son; did you ever hear of a thing called a telegraph?" and turned to take the reins of a handsome chestnut horse one of the possemen brought up to him. "Get your horses," he told the prisoners. "Get astride and let's be on the move. And men; don't get yourselves killed. There's not a man among us who wouldn't kill you in a second if you try running for it."

Marshal Withers rode up, dropped his reins and sat stonily regarding the captives. "You heard," he snarled. "Get on your damned horses."

Jubal turned, leading off. He had a knot in the pit of his stomach as heavy as a ball of pure lead, not over what had just happened, but because of what they'd done over in Libertad. That would surely come out now.

CHAPTER
SEVEN

They used up what remained of the night getting back. It was a long, long way back. They stopped twice for water and some of the men smoked, now and then, or talked a little in quiet tones, but nothing could detract from the punishing monotony of another eight hours of riding.

They reached Spencer a little before dawn. Jeff was beyond caring, or even feeling, when they entered the silent town, while his father and brother were no better off. Frank Hudson rode gloomily; he seemed the least used up, but when they were ordered curtly to dismount out front of the jailhouse, Frank's legs wobbled too.

Marshal Withers sent two possemen down to the liverybarn with those wrung-out Texas horses. He showed compassion too when he said for the word to be passed along to the liveryman to wash the backs of those Texas horses to prevent galling, and to feed them in stalls and cuff them down when they'd been grained.

Inside, the jailhouse was still hot from the day before, but it would soon cool. Then it would remain cool throughout the hottest time of day, which was perhaps the only real advantage to using adobe mud to build with.

There were two steel cages along the far wall with no intervening partition between the marshal's desk, gunrack and scattered old chairs, so that what was said inside or outside the cells would be heard by everyone in the place. In fact, the Spencer jail was just one large adobe room, flat-ceilinged and dirt-floored. It was the oldest building in town, but beyond that obvious fact, no one knew who'd built it, why, or how long ago.

The possemen crowded inside, filling the room. Marshal Wither's regarded the Pierces and Frank Hudson from a greying, exhausted face, his expression stonily hostile. Then he stepped to a bunk inside the farthest cell, grabbed a blanket and yanked it away, at the same time intently watching the faces of his prisoners.

There was a dead man upon the bunk under that blanket.

Jubal looked. So did his sons and his son-in-law. They didn't know that corpse. For a second or two it didn't dawn on them who he was, but then it did. The outlaw who failed to get out of the blasted bank in time to escape with his friends, and who'd been shot to death here in Spencer.

Jubal walked over and studied the face more closely. "What was his name?" he quietly asked Ted Withers.

"Oh hell," snorted the lawman. "As if you didn't know, you lyin' old reprobate."

From over near the door that hatless, youthful-looking older man said, "What's *your* name, oldtimer?"

Jubal turned, looking past the closed-down, hostile faces to one called Captain. "Jubal Pierce, mister. An' if I knew that dead feller I wouldn't have asked which one he was."

The hatless man kept studying old Jubal as he said, "His name was Jack Slade, oldtimer. We found a letter from someone up in Lighthill sent him down in Texas. Does the name Jack Slade mean anything to you?"

Jubal didn't answer. The name meant something to him all right, but he had no intention of saying what it was. He turned back. Jack Slade had stopped a half dozen slugs. None had struck his face or head but his chest and soft parts showed punctures.

Marshal Withers stepped across to the adjoining cage and flung back the door. "Inside," he growled. "And boys; shed your boots." When the Pierces looked up, not comprehending, Withers flintily smiled. "You're Texans; I've seen my share of boot-knives and belly-guns hidden out in the boots of men like you fellers. Step inside now, and toss out your boots."

They obeyed. When young Bob dumped his boots that two-edged knife spilled out. Several of the possemen made surprised exclamations but not Ted Withers. He stooped, retrieved the wicked weapon, and wolfishly smiled down at young Bob. "You're lucky, son. If you'd pulled that on me, I'd have cut you in two right here inside this cage."

Withers kicked aside the other boots, locked the cell and turned away. To his possemen he said, "Boys; it's late. Let's try'n snatch an hour's sleep if we can."

They all trooped out into the cool pre-dawn. One man lingered. Withers didn't protest; he simply said, "Cap; when you leave lock the door from the roadside," and ambled on out with the others.

The hatless, lanky man drew up a chair, sat down outside the cell and said, "I'm Sam Salton. I own the general store across the road."

Jubal nodded. "This here is Jeff, my eldest. That's young Bob. This here's Frank Hudson, m'son-in-law. Mind me askin' why they call you Captain?"

"That was my rank back in the war"

"I see. Captain; you was a — Confederate?"

Sam Salton nodded, watching Jubal with grave, unwavering grey eyes. "You too, oldtimer?"

"Second Texas, until we got shot all to pieces over in Louisiana. I got invalided home."

"So now you lead your sons and son-in-law robbing banks."

"No sir. I told you the Gospel truth, Captain. We weren't the ones."

"Quite a coincidence, Mister Pierce, four outlaws hit our bank. You four men knew all about it when we caught up to you. Wouldn't you call that quite a coincidence?"

"It can't be helped, Captain."

Jeff said, "Captain Salton; we were on the trail of those five men. I was the one who saw them breakin' into your bank yesterday before sunup. We took out after them. Captain; we been after those men a long while. Since they — ."

64

"Never mind all that," broke in Jubal roughly, shooting rawboned big Jeff a hard, sharp look. "Captain; that's the truth. We was after 'em, an' if we get out of here we'll still be after 'em. We'll get 'em too."

Sam Salton rubbed a hand across his square jaw looking from one prisoner to the others. "You mean you've been after those five men all the way from Texas?"

"Jeff you be quiet," said old Jubal as the older son leaned to say something. "We been after 'em a long while, Captain. A mighty long while."

"Odds were against you men. Five to four and your horses — ."

"Six," piped up young Bob. "Six to . . ." he snapped his mouth closed as all the others turned to stare.

For about five seconds no one spoke. Sam Salton finally leaned back in his rickety chair. He considered them almost benignly, almost gently, except for a gradual hard brightening of his gaze. "Now we're getting somewhere, men. Now I'm beginnin' to think I was wrong down there on the desert about you. Maybe you were tellin' the truth, Mister Pierce. Just give me one more straight answer. What happened to the sixth one?"

Jubal ponderously delved for his depleted tobacco sack, lowered his head and went to work creating a cigarette. He didn't say a word, not even after he'd lighted up and was looking through the bars at Sam Salton.

Jeff and Frank were equally as silent, their faces grim and expressionless and closed to Captain Salton. For a while longer the hatless, lanky ex-Rebel soldier sat out there gazing through at them. Then he slapped both knees with his palms and arose.

"All right, boys," he said, standing up in front of them. "I don't give a damn about your private feud. You caught up with one of them. That's all right with me. All we want is our money back."

Jubal said, "Captain; I'll tell you one more time what's as true as night follows day: me an' my boys never even seen that money. Never even thought of it. If those men hadn't hit your bank —"

"Mister Pierce," broke in Sam Salton suddenly. "How did you know, out of all the towns in New Mexico, they'd be in this one?"

Jubal hung fire over answering that. It seemed that every time a question had been asked him by this youthful-looking older man, it was a two-edged question. Old Jubal could have lied but he abhorred liars above all others, so he sat there dumbly, smoking and looking concerned, without attempting to answer.

Jeff said, in low spirits, "Hell, paw; they're going to know sooner or later. Tell him."

"You keep quiet," said the old man sharply. Then he shook his head at Captain Salton. "That's not the important thing. You're lettin' the real thieves get clean away, Captain."

Sam Salton shook his head. "Ted will send a telegram to the southerly towns. I don't think they'll get away, Mister Pierce."

66

Suddenly Salton sat down again, leaned and clasped his hands between both knees and looked closely at the four of them. He showed by the steady intentness of his expression that he no longer disbelieved old Jubal. He also showed by that same look, that he had guessed something else as well.

He said, "Boys; where did you kill him, and how?"

Jubal turned away. "We got to get some rest," he said to Frank, Jess, and young Bob. "Better make ourselves comfortable, boys," and set the example by selecting one of the pallets to sit down upon. He removed his empty shell-belt and flung it aside, punched down his hat and studiously avoided even glancing out through the boys where Sam Salton was watching his every move.

Jess and Frank and young Bob did the same, following Jubal's example. Salton slowly climbed back to his feet. He said, "Well; you're not going anywhere, boys, and remember: a telegram'll work both ways." Then he departed. They heard him lock the jailhouse door from the outside.

At once young Bob sprang up and tried the door of their cell, ran his hands over the unrelenting steel bars and turned slowly looking for a window. There was none. The only windows in this building were along the front, or roadside, wall. He swore.

"How do we bust out now; they even got my Bowie knife."

"You couldn't have used it anyway," muttered Frank, from his prone position on the floor. "Sit down, Bob."

"Sit down! Damn you Frank; you know what's goin' to happen tomorrow when one of those lousy coaches from Libertad gets here?"

"Sure I know. Sit down and relax, Bob. You're not goin' to chew your way out of here. Anyway; tomorrow's already here. Give it an hour or such a matter an' the sun'll be up again."

The youngest of them gripped the bars and strained. The steel didn't even quiver. He bent down trying to estimate the height of the bottom of their door from the floor. It was something like an inch or two. He fell to his knees and scrabbled at the flinty earth which was packed and pounded to a cement-like hardness.

Jeff said through the soft darkness. "Bob; we're not hung yet. Get some rest like Frank says. From now on we got to live each minute as it's dealt to us."

The youth whirled. His father raised up. "That's enough," he snapped, his voice sharp but also soft. It was this very softness that warned young Bob. Jubal never raised his voice; when he was on the verge of violence his voice sank to a velvety softness. His sons knew this. Bob went sulkily back to his place and sat.

"Paw; that feller Salton's the smartest one of 'em. He wangled it right out of you."

"Come the first stage," repeated Frank. "Every one of them'll know, Bob."

"We should've stayed long enough to bury him, back there in Libertad," said Jeff tiredly.

That silenced them all because it was the pure truth. If they'd buried Joe Riley they'd have bought themselves more time, but they hadn't, and whatever had prompted them to light out immediately after Riley had dropped didn't really matter now either; all that mattered was the fact that they hadn't buried him.

"Those damned scoundrels are gettin' farther away every second," groaned old Jubal. "If we get out of this we'll have it all to do over again, except from now on they'll be even harder to track down."

"If," muttered Frank from his corner. "If, Jubal. *If* we get out of this. I got a bad feelin' about it. They're goin' to know about Riley before noon today, an' they're already fired up — all but Cap'n Salton — to lynch us. Even that ox of a town marshal. I don't see a whole lot of hope, do you?"

"Sure, boy," said Jubal quietly, "I'm older. As long as you can breathe, you can hope. I've been in bad spots before and I'm still here."

"This bad, Jubal? With two-thirds of a whole comunity crazy to strangle you? I doubt it. There's a sight of difference between fighting soldiers who got nothing personal against a man. They'll only kill you in battle, otherwise they'll throw you in a stockade somewhere and feed you mealy gruel. This is different. Remember; Joe Riley was known over in the Libertad country."

"We'll have to tell them the truth eventually," put in taciturn Jeff.

"I got a feelin' about that too," stated Frank. "You heard how Salton talked down there when the others'd have shot us. He's a law-abidin' man. Murder's murder to him, and you seen that he packs a heap of weight in

69

this country. Even that city marshal backs off when Sam Salton speaks."

"Go to sleep," murmured Jubal, hiding his face from them. "This isn't helpin' any, lyin' awake diggin' our own graves with words. We'll go on hoping."

For perhaps ten minutes none of them spoke. The pre-dawn chill completely cooled their jailhouse residence. A noisy young rooster with a changing voice crowed lustily to make a little break in the stillness. One of them sat up and made a cigarette, propped his heavy shoulders against the adobe back-wall and smoked in stolid silence. That was Frank, least worried, it seemed, of them all.

Outside, a thin, weak pinkness came steadily down across the eastward desert. It caught rising dust behind an early coach travelling the roadway from the east, from over at Libertad where it had picked up one passenger, two sacks of mail, and had left town while it was still dark over there. Aside from this solitary moving vehicle though, the land still lay undisturbed.

Frank finished his smoke, drew up both knees, hooked thick arms around them and put his chin down atop the knees. He couldn't sleep. "Jubal," he said softly, "you awake?"

"I'm awake, Frank."

"One time Maria told me — she said: 'Frank; we'll build up this ranch and have children to leave it to.'"

"Go to sleep, Frank."

CHAPTER
EIGHT

It was nine o'clock when Ted Withers brought their breakfast. He didn't say a word. Not a single word. He looked at them with a chilly, impersonal stare, and gestured for them to line up against the back wall. After they'd complied he unlocked the door, shoved in their trays, backed off and locked the door again. Then he stood watching for a moment, stony-faced and as silent as a statue, before walking over to his desk and tossing down some mail he'd been packing in his rear pocket.

They ate in silence, tousled, sore-eyed from desert dust, dispirited, but hungry. Afterwards they piled their tin plates next to the door and lit up. The town was noisy outside. They could hear wagons grinding through the dust, horsemen trotting past, dogs and children on the move, and none of it touched them, was in any way related to them.

At ten o'clock Sam Salton walked in accompanied by a tall, decidedly Mexican-looking man but whose skin despite its layers of suntan, was fair. Marshal Withers nodded without getting up; he'd obviously known these two were coming and just as obviously didn't approve of something they were doing.

Captain Salton caught at the chair he'd used earlier and swung it to drop down astraddle the thing, long arms hooked across the back. The tall, half-blood Mexican hooked thumbs in his shell-belt and curiously studied each of the Pierces, and Frank Hudson, in turn. After he seemed quite satisfied about something he said in accent-less English. "Well; we found him right where you fellers left him — five bullets in his back. Which one of you shot him twice?"

Jubal leaned upon the south wall of his cell examining the furry tip of his smoke as though the tall Mexican and Sam Salton didn't exist. Frank looked out at them from his blank face while rawboned big Jeff and young Bob kept their faces averted.

"You're not helpin' any," said Sam Salton quietly, and Jubal dropped a look upon him.

"Any reason why we should help, Cap'n?"

"I think so, Mister Pierce. It was self-defence wasn't it — until you cut him down?"

Jubal's eyes gradually widened. Jeff and Bob looked up. Frank, the cigarette half way to his lips, held it like that, studying Sam Salton from unblinking eyes.

The tall Mexican reached under his vest and drew forth a sixgun. From a wooden face he said, "Here's his gun, boys; four shots out of it. The wonder's that he didn't clip one of you. Joe Riley was a fast man with a gun — and an accurate one." He paused, gazed at the gun he was holding, then slowly put his dark stare upon old Jubal. "Mister; correct me if I'm wrong. The way I traced it out after some kids found his body north of town, is that he saw you four riding towards him. He recognized you. He got behind that tree and when you were within range he opened on you. Then he panicked when you split up and made a run on him. He turned and run — and you fellers cut him down."

The tall Mexican's wooden expression didn't change one bit but his dark eyes showed a hard slyness. Frank stood up, dropped his smoke and stamped on it with his head down. He said, "You're right good at readin' sign, mister. Mind tellin' us who you are?"

"Town Marshal of Libertad, *amigo*; the name is Juan Turcio."

Frank nodded. He understood and exchanged a wise, long look with Turcio. They understood perfectly. So did Jubal and Jeff and young Bob, but it took them slightly longer.

From over at his desk Ted Withers twisted around. "Juan; they still shot him in the back. You said that yourself." Withers was indignant; he was also upset over having been proven incorrect in assuming the Pierces and Hudson were the bank robbers.

Turcio didn't even look over his shoulders; he kept staring straight at old Jubal as he answered. "Ted; how the hell else do you bring down a stinking rat like Joe Riley who fires on you from ambush, then runs?"

Withers whipped forward turning his angry back to them all again. Turcio went over and tossed the heavy pistol on Withers's desk. Then he walked back and stood as before, both thumbs hooked into his shell-belt, gazing impassively into the cell. Sam Salton hadn't said a thing; now he unfolded his arms and stood up. He and Juan Turcio were the same build and lanky height.

"Looks like we should've listened to you down on the desert, Mister Pierce," he said. "Those men of mine I left down there to look around got back a few minutes ago riding hard most of the night."

Jubal's interest quickened. "They found the tracks?"

"No, Mister Pierce. They found the men. One of my men came back tied belly-down across his horse."

"Dead?" breathed old Jubal.

Salton nodded. "The other one gave us a good description though. We've sent wires to the border towns."

Frank moved towards the front of the cell. "Captain," he asked, "do we get out of here now?"

Ted Withers slammed down his pencil over at the desk and angrily arose, eyes flashing. "*I'm* the law here," he roared. "*I* say whether you get out or not!"

Frank stood briefly silent, looking into the distorted, splotchy face across the room. In the same quiet tone he then repeated his question, addressing it to the stiff-standing, majestically angry town marshal.

Withers gave no prompt reply nor did his stiffness depart right away. He said, "Juan; how could you be so damned sure about all this? You said yourself kids tramped all over around Riley's body, and some fellers from town also rode out there."

Juan Turcio turned, bracing into Withers' fury, his voice low-pitched. "Come on, Ted; what you tryin' to do? There's Riley's damned gun; look at it. You know better'n think I can't read the sign even when some kids and fools on horseback muss it up a little." Turcio shook his head at Ted Withers. "You're helpin' those

74

bank robbers, makin' all this lousy delay. I told you I'd ride with you after them. But if you're goin' to act like this, the hell with it."

Sam Salton watched and listened, and finally mediated. "Turn them out, Ted, and let's get going."

Withers glared. "Sure. An' next you'll want them to ride with us!"

Sam Salton's answer came right back. "If they want to come along, I'm for letting them. After all, Ted, they'd have caught those outlaws if we hadn't loused them up."

"You mean me, don't you, Sam?"

Salton's grey gaze began to harden towards the town marshal but otherwise he showed no rising anger. Even his voice was the same when he said, "Ted; you were the one who heard them talking and led us forward to stalk them. You were the one who refused to detach any possemen, so I had to send my two men. Now Ted, I don't give a copper-coloured damn how you feel over all this, but I'm going to tell you one thing: when a man's bad wrong and is too stubborn to admit it, I begin losing patience with him. Now let's have an end to this. Let these men out and let's get the hell to riding."

Ted Withers stood stiffly erect staring at Captain Salton. He had the appearance of someone who'd just been slapped. Without another word he turned, opened the door and looked out towards the tie-rack. There were two saddled horses out there, each with a carbine slung under the *rosadero* and with one tight-rolled blanket behind the cantle. He turned back.

"Just us?" he asked, looking surprised.

"Juan and you an' me," said Captain Salton. "It was Juan's idea."

"No dust and we ride faster that way," put in the town marshal from Libertad. "Besides; by the time we get down along the border someone'll have spotted them; they'll be locked up for us."

Withers glanced out into the warming-up morning roadway again. "I'll go fetch my horse," he said, and would have hiked on out but Salton stopped him.

"The keys, Ted."

Withers jerked his head and resumed moving. "On the desk."

When Salton walked across to get the cell-lock keys Juan Turcio raised a finger and lightly lay it across his lips, facing towards the cell and away from Sam Salton, then he stepped aside and ignored the prisoners until after Captain Salton had freed them.

"Well," said Salton, reaching into a pocket. "You boys deserve at least a couple of free meals and a good night's rest at the expense of the town of Spencer." He held out some money towards old Jubal.

Frank Hudson said, "We'll pick up some grub at the store, Captain, then get some fresh animals at the liverybarn an' be right with you."

Juan Turcio faintly nodded, impassively watching the Texans with his dark, steady gaze. Sam Salton, though, scowled. "You men've been in the saddle too long already. Mister Pierce; you're not a young man any more."

76

"I got m'reasons for this," stated old Jubal. "Bob; you'n Frank go fetch us animals from the liverybarn. Jeff; step across the way and fetch some tins of food. And Jeff; maybe an extra box of ca'tridges for the hand-guns."

As the younger men began moving Sam Salton reached for Jeff's arm. "Wait; it's my store over there. I'll go with you. No charge for whatever you want." Salton and Jeff Pierce reached the door before Salton paused, twisting. "Juan . . .?" he called.

"Go on, Sam. I'll wait here where it's cool."

The others all left. Jubal lifted off his hat, ran bent fingers through his matted hair and said, "We're obliged to you, Mister Turcio. You don't have to explain anythin'."

The tall, light-skinned, dark-eyed man's lips lifted in a sardonic quirk. "You were at the house. My wife described all of you but the youngest one. I'm not a good peace officer, Mister Pierce. That's only my part-time job anyway. By trade I buy an' sell livestock. As for the rest of it — I didn't know Joe Riley was alive; that he was coming back."

"You don't have to say any more, Mister Turcio."

"Yes I do. I've got to tell you I fired those four shots out of Riley's gun, then high-tailed it over here in case you'd come this way, to try'n catch the four of you and say — it wasn't murder — it was just execution."

"Well; like I said, Mister Turcio, we're real obliged to you."

The tall, younger man gave his head a little shake and reached up to thumb back his hat. "I'm being

77

honest with you. You be the same with me. Joe Riley made love to my wife when I was on the trail a year back. That's my reason for helping those who saved me from being a murderer too. I give you my word, I'd have done it exactly the same way. Now then — why did you kill him?"

"There were six of them, Mister Turcio. They raided and plundered down into Deaf Smith County, Texas."

"They robbed you?"

"They killed my two daughters, Mister Turcio. The youngest was barely eighteen. Her sister was Frank Hudson's wife. She was twenty-four and looked exactly like her dead mother."

Juan Turcio stood in slow thought. "Killed them," he murmured. "I can imagine how." He pushed out a sinewy hand. "I already told you — I'm a lousy law officer — I got too much feeling to ever be a good one. An' now I'm a liar as well for helpin' murderers. And Mister Pierce, as God is above me, I'd do it the same way tomorrow all over again. You want to shake hands with a man who lies and helps murderers?"

Old Jubal stonily shook the tall man's hand thinking a bitter thought: never say what you won't do, because sooner or later if you live long enough, Fate will surely make you do it. He, who detested liars above all other pariahs, had just shaken the hand of a liar.

"It's a pretty cruel world at times, Mister Turcio, an' for an old man it gets more an' more complicated all the time. If anybody'd ever told me I'd have deliberately shot a man to death — in the back — I'd have challenged him. Yet I got to tell you the answer to somethin' you asked a while back: it was me shot him twice."

Juan Turcio nodded and let his breath out, then turned towards the door where he could see Jeff and Sam Salton emerging from the general store over across the way. "Mister Pierce; you got to be wiser'n me because you've lived a sight longer, but I'll tell you something I learned last year when I went huntin' Joe Riley to shoot him. There's a big difference between law and justice. The law that Ted Withers serves says no man's ever got the right to kill another man for revenge. Justice says different." Turcio turned back to old Jubal. "That's what I meant when I said I make a lousy peace officer, Mister Pierce. I believe more in justice than I do in law. I reckon you're the same."

Jubal, who'd never found this answer by himself, stood thoughtful for a spell, until Jeff sang out to him from outside. Then he raised his face and smiled at Juan Turcio. "You put it just right, Mister Turcio. Just exactly right. And I tell you, you just lifted a heavy weight off a man's spirit." He nodded. "I'm right obliged to you. I said that before, but this time I mean it more'n ever."

Juan Turcio's dark eyes softened a little. "We'd better get out there. The others'll be back with the horses soon."

There was heat in the air now. Noon wasn't too far off. Little bands of townsmen stood bunched like sheep here and there along both sides of the roadway as Marshal Withers came leading his horse from out back. It was a different animal than the one he'd put all those miles on the night before. He avoided looking directly at Sam Salton, but that was the only indication he offered to show that his indignation hadn't entirely died away yet.

Farther down, Bob and Frank were each astride, leading another saddled animal between them for Jubal. They were all rigged out with their own equipment, right down to the booted carbines, but the horses were different; fresher and stronger-looking.

Sam Salton wore his sixgun high and with the butt turned cross-ways. He was the only one among them who used this border-draw. All the others wore their guns the traditional way, slung low, tied down, butts to the rear. Salton also carried a rifle in the boot instead of a carbine, which was different from the others, but as everyone mounted up, no one made any comment. What mattered wasn't how a man wore his gun, but rather how he used it when the critical time came. Salton led them out of town in a slow little mile-eating lope.

CHAPTER
NINE

Sam Salton knew the country. He also knew where he was going. When Jubal inquired, Salton told him that his surviving man had explained exactly where the outlaws had been when Salton's two men had stumbled onto them. "I know a quicker way to reach that waterhole too, which is the way we're heading now."

After that they had little to say. Marshal Withers made a point out of avoiding the faces of his ex-prisoners. He didn't have much to say to any of them for the first three hours. It seemed to take him that long to get the embers put out inside him.

It was pretty much as it had been the day before; the heat, alkali-dust that galled the throat and stung the eyes, monotonous riding over a landscape that changed very little mile after mile.

Sam Salton evidently knew every waterhole and every stone trough because they were never completely thirsty and their shirts never completely dried before they came to another place to douse one another. To old Jubal, Salton became what he'd obviously once been, an army officer. Jubal even addressed him as sir, and once when Salton objected, Jubal just shrugged.

"A man learns lessons a heap easier'n he un-learns 'em — Sir."

Juan Turcio and rawboned Jeff rode together. Bringing up the rear were Frank Hudson and young Bob. The youth hadn't yet figured out all the details of their release from jail, but when he'd ask Frank, the only answer he'd get would be a dark scowl and a headshake. Frank obviously — and properly — thought there'd be a time for all this to be discussed, and this definitely wasn't that time.

When dusk began settling they stopped to eat. Salton had two cans of condensed milk which he mixed with water from a trough. They all drank the stuff gratefully even though it tasted like nothing a genuine cow would ever lay claim to.

They also had tinned beef and some tinned fruit. Jubal gravely informed the others that he hadn't been used to eating that good, even back home in Deaf Smith County.

That was Ted Withers's opening to ask a pointed question. "What have these men we're after done to you, Mister Pierce?"

"They murdered two girls, Marshal," murmured the old man, stabbing fruit in a tin with his pocketknife. "Mauled them, then murdered them."

"Relatives of yours?"

Frank Hudson's eyes widened on Marshal Withers. "They were his daughters, an' if you got any more questions, keep them to yourself!"

Withers straightened up where he sat but Sam Salton leaned far over and held forth a can of peaches. "Will you tell me, Ted, why in hell they never can put these blasted things up without first takin' out the pips? Here; you eat 'em. I think I cracked a tooth."

Juan Turcio kept his head down as he ate, but he had no trouble at all sensing the troubled atmosphere as he said, "Ted; men have their good reasons for sacrifice, every time. Let's just leave it like that for now."

They rode on after eating with a slightly thicker moon at their backs and above them. When the coolness came, slowly and miserly at first, stronger and sweeter as the night wore along, they had trouble remaining awake. It wasn't just the riding though, it was also the food. To help, Sam engaged old Jubal in conversation about the war. They hadn't served in the same theatres, but they'd served a common cause which was more than enough to keep their reminiscences going on and on.

Turcio and Jeff talked of Texas, of horses and also of graded-up breeds of cattle. They discussed horses they'd known the way professional horsemen do, rather like some men discuss women they've known.

Frank though, was back deep down in his silence again. When young Bob would drowsily say something, Frank was deaf. For the youngest among them the ride became torment; like youth anywhere on earth, the vivacity, the effervescence, was there, but the oaken stamina which only came with age, was entirely lacking. Bob dropped to sleep from time to time and jerked back wide awake when instinct told him he'd drop out of the saddle.

They made their longest halt below where the circular trough had been; far enough down-country to be verging on an area none of the men with old Jubal had seen before. It was down here where Sam Salton unerringly led them to a genuine cold-water spring in the midst of a desolate stretch of desert where no sane man would ever expect water to lie.

There were the marks of others having been here not too long before. Ted Withers went around looking at the discarded cans, at the imprints of men's bodies against the dusty earth, and grunting to himself. This, obviously, was where the bank robbers had been in camp when Salton's two men had stumbled upon them, but it was too dark to read much sign.

They smoked and rested the horses. Young Bob fell asleep. Jubal lay back when he'd finished his cigarette. Jeff lay back leaving only Frank sitting with the two lawmen and Sam Salton.

Turcio said, "They'll hit the first town where the river bends east, down a ways. My guess is that they're down there now, trying to drink the place dry."

"We'd have had them," muttered Frank without lifting his eyes.

Ted Withers looked sharply across at Hudson. He evidently thought Frank's remark had been a gouge at him. But he wisely kept his peace.

"We'll get them," said Salton, yawning and stretching out upon the gritty earth. "You'll get your sleep while we're doing it, too."

Frank didn't comprehend. "How?" he demanded.

84

"The first town's called Dolores. There is a coach line connecting all the towns down along the border. We'll leave the horses at Dolores and take the stage until we find them. It's hard sleeping on a stage, but you men'll have no trouble doing it."

Frank continued to watch Sam Salton. He had a capable way about him. He made decisions with ease and came up with the right answers every time. Obviously, Sam Salton had been a good soldier. Frank said, "Then what do we do with 'em — Captain?"

Salton's answer was drowsy. "That'll be up to them, Mister Hudson. But I've got a feeling they won't put up their hands."

"They won't get that chance," mumbled Frank.

Ted Withers, in the act of scooping out a place in the sand for his hips before lying back, stopped and turned. He looked straight at Frank, his brows rolling down. He might have said something but Juan Turcio asked him a question, and threw Withers off in that fashion.

"How do we get four of them back to Spencer, Ted?"

Withers pondered that. "Rent horses at Dolores, I reckon. There's no other way."

Juan Turcio nodded. He'd known the answer before he'd asked the question, but the question had done what he'd proposed; it had avoided a clash between Hudson and Withers. "That'll cost the county more good money," he said, and lay back.

"What do you figure we should do, Juan, lynch 'em?"

Frank spoke up. "Last night, Mister Withers, you were pretty close to doing that to us."

Withers let all his breath out and didn't stir. The ground was warm and dusty-soft. In a weary tone he said, "It didn't happen, Mister Hudson. That's all that really matters. It didn't happen."

They were all sleeping except Juan Turcio. He sat and smoked and watched the moon move in inch at a time across their lonely firmament, lost in droll, private thoughts which brought no smile to his long lips and no warmth to his sober dark eyes. He secretly thought, of them all including the four murderers, he was by far the worst man, yet this didn't bother him very much. After all, as he'd explained it to Jubal Pierce, the only wrong which had been done had been committed against an abstraction called "Law". Juan Turcio, like most frontiersmen, saw hardly any relationship between law and what was just and right. The killing of Joe Riley was as right as anything Juan Turcio knew of. Still and all, in the eyes of the law, he was the worst man among his companions. He finally smiled over that to himself and put aside his hat. Life was hard to understand at its simplest. When men began forging order and standardized sequence out of it, all that happened was worse disorder and less standardization. When a man is yoked to convention he ceases to be a man. As he eased back, Juan Turcio thought that those who fought hardest for independence were the least independent of all living creatures; what they really fought over was which of several systems of innocuous servitude should triumph, never for individual freedom, or they wouldn't fight as orderly, organized armies, but rather as individual men.

Juan Turcio got the least sleep, unless it was Frank Hudson who achieved this but none of the others knew whether Frank slept or not and he most certainly didn't volunteer any such information.

Jeff and Sam Salton awoke about the same time, roused the others then went after the horses. It was still night. When the animals were led up everyone was ready. Not loudly laughing exactly, over the prospect of what lay ahead, but nevertheless ready to get on with it.

Salton rode up front again, but this time old Jubal rode stirrup with him. They said nothing. Neither did any of the others until Bob grumbled something back at the tail-end of the little column and was growled at by Frank.

At least it was cool, and if that seemed to be a minor blessing it wasn't, because daytime heat was more demoralizing than lack of sleep or the growing suspicion in some of their minds that failure lay at the end of this punishing ride. Regardless of where those outlaws were by this time — and it certainly wouldn't be anywhere close by — they wouldn't remain there long, and every time they moved from now on, would be farther and farther from the Spencer country.

They crossed the balance of the desert before sunup, came down where the Pajaro River crossed, and after that, southward, found a green and productive land. Mexican homes stood here and there in the midst of growing crops of one kind and another, which proved less than Mexicans were industrious, which they weren't, and it proved more that the desert, barren and desolate and worthless as it seemed, would transform itself into a rich world, once ample water was trickled over it.

"The town's yonder," explained Sam Salton, pointing where first daylight was tinting a little jumble of adobe blocks several miles ahead. "They won't still be here, of course, but they'll be remembered and we'll take up the trail from that."

Salton was correct. Even though when he and his gaunt companions on their tucked-up horses rode in before full daylight, a Mexican hostler down at Dolores's solitary liverybarn recalled with no effort the four men who'd come reeling out of the desert.

"They slept from mid-day until nine o'clock, then they drank from evening until midnight, *Señores*, then they come here, got their horses and started over towards Castroville."

Sam Salton told the hostler to put up their horses, to cuff them off, feed them well, and put each of them inside the barn not outside in a corral. He then led the way up to a little café next door to the stage depot, and pushed in off the empty boardwalk just as the proprietor was going back behind his counter after opening that door for the morning trade.

The caféman was startled. So many customers so early was unheard of, apparently, or else their sunken-eyed, stony-faced look and travel-stained, grim appearance, put him instantly in mind of outlaws, for he stood over at the far corner of his counter, mouth agape.

"Start out with plenty of coffee," called Sam Salton. "And after that, *amigo*, how about *huevos* for everyone, some fried steak, maybe, some *frijoles*?"

The caféman came to life like a monkey on a string. He began jerking his head up and down. "*Si, si*," he beamed. "*Si, mi jefe.* Right away; esfried eggs, esfried steak, an' esfried beans. Coffee comin' first."

The man scuttled into his kitchen. They could hear him busily slamming pans around, kicking the grate on his stove, cursing when he inadvertently grabbed the coffee-pot handle without first wrapping his apron around it.

"How far is Castroville?" asked Jeff. He directed the question to Sam Salton but Ted Withers answered.

"Ten, twelve miles, and it looks just like Dolores." Marshal Withers had evidently been thinking, for he said, "They'll rest longer an' start stayin' longer pretty soon. So far I don't figure they know we're after them."

Frank Hudson looked up. "What of the two men of Captain Salton's who stumbled onto them?"

Withers shook his head. "Naw; just two men'd make 'em think Salton's boys were maybe more outlaws or possibly a pair of woodticks who herded sheep or something down on the desert. Who'd expect two men who bumbled right into an outlaw camp without knowing it was there, to be a full-fledged posse?"

That made some sense. Even Frank nodded, and watched the Mex caféman come around with their cups and pour them full. "When will he catch up?" he asked. Withers replied to that too.

"They'll slow down from here on. It's my guess we'll hit them maybe by tomorrow night or the next day."

Sam Salton said nothing. Neither did old Jubal. When their platters came they lit into the food as though this might be their last meal for a long time. Either the caféman was an excellent cook or they were very hungry, or perhaps both, because when they finished they were looking a lot less grim. Each of them had a second cup of java, then they all trooped back outside where sunlight was brightening the whole place now.

They went next door to the stage office, ascertained a coach would be pulling out within a few minutes for Castroville, and sat down on wall-benches to wait. Their punishment was largely over now; as Captain Salton had said, they could sleep, keep up the pursuit, and gain their badly-needed rest now, at the same time. Even grim Frank and tired-looking old Jubal, looked satisfied at how things were turning out.

CHAPTER
TEN

The heat down in this green country wasn't less, the humidity was more. If that didn't make a whole lot of sense to travellers from the east, it made sense to the Texans and their companions, for although they were drenched with sweat before they ever reached Castroville, nevertheless the process of dehydration was slowed considerably and there was no painful dryness to nostrils, eyes and throat.

They slept on the stage like drugged men, crowded inside like penned-up sheep, with their saddles tied atop the coach and their guns inside on the floor. It wasn't comfortable, sleeping like that, but at this point their systems didn't require anything more than just slumber.

When the coach stopped mid-way to water the horses at a roadside trough, they all piled out to shake the kinks out and look around. Northward, the land was still watered by the Pajaro, but southward as far, and probably much farther, as the eye could see, was more desert wasteland. Somewhere down there, unmarked and ignored, lay the U.S.-Mexican boundary line. Someday there would be smartly-uniformed patrols, white stone markers, a prickly pride on both sides, but right now this was far from the case. Mexican nationals wandered up into New Mexico Territory with total ease; sometimes doing it even when they had no idea they'd crossed over. Also, other men crossed that invisible line when they knew perfectly well what they were doing. They were the outlaws of both nations.

And the Army, the Texas Rangers, U.S. lawmen and Mexican *Rurales* — rural constabulary patrols who were Mexican law unto themselves and very rarely ever burdened themselves with prisoners — skirmished on both sides of the line with outlaws, wherever they encountered them. U.S. outlaws were only safe from U.S. lawmen deep inside Mexico in one of the little villages down there. Then, though, it wasn't a matter of any certainty that they were south of the border that made the Mexicans willing to fight to keep U.S. lawmen out, it was Mexican nationalism which had its good reasons for wishing to chase U.S. troops and peace officers back up into New Mexico.

What troubled Jubal, and he mentioned it at the way-stop while the horses were being watered and the driver was smoking his mid-morning cigarette, was that once the outlaws they were chasing found out pursuit was close behind, they would turn straight southward and dodge their way down over the line.

Jeff's comment was simple. "Then we'll go down there after them."

Ted Withers looked less than enthusiastic and Juan Turcio smiled at him. "We'll get in and out all right," he told the other lawman. "But first we'll have to find some walnut dye for your hide, Ted."

No one laughed. The driver waited a few moments after his horses had tanked up, then killed his smoke and signalled for the passengers to climb back inside. "Not much farther," he said.

They rolled again, their coach rocking from side to side as well as continuing its backwards-forwards lurching. Many a stage passenger had become sick from this motion, but the men riding towards Castroville inside this particular stage had other things on their minds.

"What comes after Castroville?" asked Frank Hudson of Ted Withers.

"Daggett. Not so many greasers around the Daggett country. Not so much water either. The river cuts southward down into Mexico between Castroville and Daggett." Marshal Withers yawned and stretched powerful arms, then slumped, gazing out the window where a not-too-consistent landscape rocked by.

Jubal slept again. So did Sam Salton and Juan Turcio. Young Bob half slept. He'd awaken from time to time when they'd hit a particularly bad chuckhole, then look briefly around and drop off again. Jeff smoked and thought and finally asked Withers something they'd rarely discussed on the trail. "How much damage did that explosion do to your bank, back in Spencer, Marshal?"

"Enough, damn their lousy hides," exclaimed Withers. "Busted the safe and broke every scantlin' in the north wall where the safe stood. Broke every window anywhere close by and blew the roadside doors clean off the front wall. Maybe it did more damage but

I didn't get to make much of an investigation. Roger Small, the president of our bank, said he was afraid the building might've been too badly weakened to be safe, now."

"How come Jack Slade got to be trapped in there?"

"I don't know. He was knocked silly by the explosion I reckon. When I got over there he was stumblin' around like a drunk man. All the others were gone, but this Slade. When he seen the townsmen coming he yelled something, then started shooting." Withers shrugged. "They'd have killed him anyway; by the time everyone who owned a gun was out there. They poured enough lead into the bank to suffocate him."

"And the money?"

Wither's face was briefly shadowed with a look of pain. "I had four hundred in savings in there. Altogether, they got nine thousand. Cap Salton lost most of it; at least he lost the biggest share."

Jeff inhaled, exhaled, and thoughtfully said, "Then they'll have all the money they'd need to buy their way to safety, if they figure that's necessary. They robbed another bank over eastward a hundred miles or so; we heard about that on the trail. Then there'd be the other robberies along the way." He looked at Withers. "It's about time for 'em to call quits and split up."

"I sure hope not," Withers said fervently. "If they scatter we'll be forever runnin' them down, one at a time."

Jeff didn't reply to that. He and his kinsmen knew the town every one of those surviving renegades was from, and while that was no guarantee the outlaws would return to those places, it was enough to get a fresh start from, if it came to that in this chase. But Jeff had no intention of telling Marshal Withers any of this. As far as he was concerned, he'd have much preferred doing this without any lawmen along, unless perhaps it was Juan Turcio, in whom Jeff had faith as an individual man, not as a peace officer.

They reached Castroville right at high noon. As the driver had intimated, along with Sam Salton, it wasn't much different from Dolores. They left their saddlery parked in the stage office and crossed to the rooming-house to get baths, shaves, and to afterwards come together again outside that building on the shaded plank-walk for a little discussion. Sam Salton suggested they do exactly what old Jubal had put his kinsmen to doing when they'd first arrived back in Spencer.

"Wander around, ask questions, try and pick up the trail. Juan and I'll be over at the jailhouse if you find anything or need us. We know the local town marshal."

Ted Withers paired off with young Bob for some reason, but there'd never been any fondness between those two, which left Jeff and Frank and Jubal to amble off apart from the others.

Castroville had a preponderantly Mexican population, but there was also a scattering of lean Texans, mostly rangemen or wild-horse trappers — possibly outlaws too — as well as the customary nondescript gamblers, floaters, drifters and whatnot that inhabited border towns. Its buildings were all of adobe, usually with walls a yard thick, flat roofs, and the town had several *cantinas*.

It was in one of those latter places — named The Trinity, which would have shocked most Americans except for the fact that Mexicans, by and large being good Catholics, had a habit of naming even saloons after church symbols — that Jubal picked up a scrap of interesting information.

"Sure," said the Texan who ran The Trinity *cantina*. "I saw those four. Plenty wrung out too, an' plenty loaded with money. They was around until last night, then three of 'em pulled out. I know they did because I was out back gettin' some fresh air and seen 'em ridin' on over towards Daggett. They were carryin' a load, too, but not so drunk they couldn't sit their saddles."

"Only three?" asked Jubal, and leaned across the bar watching the Texan. "What of the fourth one?"

"Dunno, *amigo*. Maybe he's still around." The Texan broadly smiled and dropped one raffish eyelid. "We got some almighty fancy *señoritas* around Castroville, an' them boys looked like they'd been a long while away from civilization."

Jubal strolled outside and waited for Frank and Jeff to join him. He related what the barman had said, then all three of them headed down to the local *calabozo*.

The marshal of Castroville wasn't in town but he'd left a deputy, a cowboy named Troy Beeman, to mind things, or, as Beeman said, acting worried in the face of genuine trouble impending, "I'm just sort of supposed to keep the drunks from gettin' run over by wagons an' to keep fellers from thumpin' hell out of one another.

I've never had to face up to no wanted outlaws before, when I've helped out."

He'd heard what Jubal related, and didn't like the prospects it offered. Neither did he know anything about four strangers in Castroville, but he said riders came and went, sometimes heading southward over the line, sometimes heading eastward towards Texas.

"If they don't cause no harm here, the marshal don't brother 'em, an' neither do I."

Ted and young Bob came along, were told by Jeff what the barman had reported to old Jubal, and were ready for the search then and there. It was Jubal who was being deliberate now. They didn't know, actually, whether the renegade was still in town, but assuming that he was, they didn't know where to start looking, unless of course someone would recall the name of some girl their renegade had gone home with.

Sam Salton agreed. The thing to do, he thought, was circulate around singly, asking more questions. Juan Turcio and Ted Withers said they'd accompany the youthful deputy town marshal; that the deputy's prestige — or at least his badge — might help them to get the answer they wanted.

They broke up again, leaving the jailhouse one at a time until only the lawmen were still in there. Jubal, the last one to depart, said if they could find the man, determine which outlaw he was, and take him alive, it would probably help them find the other three.

It was nearly two o'clock. The heat was past its zenith but it was still hot enough out to fry eggs on a piece of iron without any fire beneath it. Even so, however, the residents of Castroville were amply in evidence. Being largely of Mexican descent, they were more or less indifferent to the heat. Even the Americans among them, such as the Texans, had also lived their full lives in this blast-furnace summertime atmosphere and didn't regard it as any definite obstacle, if they had anything which needed to be done out in it.

There was the customary haze, far out. Castroville's sidewalks, like most walkways in the Southwestern cow towns, had wooden awnings overhead to shield pedestrians. It was in this more pleasant atmosphere that merchants often placed benches outside their store, undoubtedly in the hope of attracting customers, but also simply to enable people to sit in shade, a precious commodity in any desert country.

Troy Beeman, who knew just about everyone in the countryside, told Withers and Turcio that if anyone knew any juicy gossip, it'd be the oldsters who perched on those benches all day long, whittling, gossiping, and expectorating amber juice over into the roadway dust. They saw everything, knew everyone, and could be counted upon even though the wanted man had perhaps made his date after nightfall, to have already heard of it even though they didn't loaf on the roadway benches after suppertime.

The trouble was, that although the cantankerous old men probably knew, they weren't free with their information. Juan, Ted Withers and the deputy town marshal had to buy drinks for six different old gaffers before one came up with anything at all.

"I see things," he told Troy Beeman, suspiciously eyeing the two travel-stained men with Beeman. "But boy; how you figure I lived this long?"

Juan looked over their heads at Ted. The two strangers strolled off a few yards down the bar and had a beer by themselves. "If I was that old," growled Withers, "I wouldn't be afraid of someone finding out I tipped the law and come gunning for me."

Juan Turcio said, "Ted; if you were a hundred and fifty you'd be straining just as hard to reach one hundred and fifty-one as that old man is straining to reach eighty. Life is sweeter the older you get an' the more uncertain you are about what comes next."

Beeman left the oldster and came over looking grave. "He seen him all right. It cost me another whiskey to get it out of him though. Why in hell won't those old men just drink beer that costs a nickel; why's it always got to be two-bit whiskey?"

"Makes the blood boil quicker," muttered Withers. "All right; what did he see?"

"A stranger go off towards the back of town with a girl everyone knows named Elena Gardea."

"Garcia?" asked Juan, looking faintly perplexed.

"No. Not Garcia — Gardea."

"Mexican?"

Troy Beeman got impatient. "What the hell difference does it make? Anyway; I know where she lives. It's a *jacal* over on the east side of town."

Withers drained off the last of his beer, dragged a beefy paw across his mouth and turned. "Maybe it's a wild goose chase, but let's go. If it's our man, we'll nail his damned hide to the wall."

"We better get the others," said Beeman, anxious again. "I'll feel a sight better if that Salton feller's along."

They went back outside. The old man who'd traded them their information for the shots of whiskey acted as though they didn't exist. He was whittling on a length of willow, and looking darkly resentful of something.

The lawmen split up to go search for the Pierces and Frank Hudson. They were to meet back at the jailhouse. As they departed the old man stopped whittling to look with candid rancour after all of them. He evidently, in his lifetime, had come to a firm conviction regarding lawmen. All lawmen. But he resumed the whittling without leaving his bench, so whether he disliked lawmen or not, evidently he disliked outlaws even more, or he'd have gone to warn one.

CHAPTER
ELEVEN

Jubal and his kinsmen weren't hard to locate. They were standing together outside that same *cantina* where old Jubal had picked up that scrap of interesting information, discussing something else. Frank had also found out the girl's name, but not from the barman who evidently didn't know for a fact that the wanted man had actually gone off with a girl, but instead from a *vaquero*, a Mexican cowboy who worked for cow outfits on both sides of the line, and who'd been courting Elena Gardea.

This *vaquero*, his wild jealousy nearly burnt down to coals by the time Frank came onto the man, was already half drunk when he poured out his soul to Hudson. The girl, it seemed, or so at least the *vaquero* claimed, had milked him of his wages, had sent him out to make more money, and had then turned her back on him in contempt when this *Yanqui* had come along, only because the *Yanqui* had plenty of money in his pockets.

"Probably a *pistolero*," complained the *vaquero* to Frank. "*El bandido*. I tried to warn her. To tell her he was a bad one, *mala hombre*. You know what she tol' me, *amigo*? To go hit my mother. Me! She tol' me that,

101

after I worked hard to give her things, and money, and to make my love on her. How do you think for that, *amigo*?"

Frank had been cold. He'd said, "What's his name, or didn't she tell you?"

"She tol' me, *amigo*. His name is Pat Potter. He's a big cowman over around Albuquerque." The *vaquero* threw back his head to silently grimace in derision. "Big cowman — hah! He's an outlaw!"

Frank's sunken gaze lingered briefly on the *vaquero*, not in pity surely, and not in scorn entirely, then he'd walked off and found the others, and told them what he knew.

That was when the lawmen came strolling up in company with Castroville's deputy town marshal. The name Pat Potter meant nothing to Salton, Withers, Turcio or the deputy town marshal, but it meant something to the Pierces and Frank Hudson.

"He'll be gone," mumbled young Bob. "Deputy; you lead off. At least this Elena Gardea'll know which way he went an' how much lead he's got on us."

Beeman wordlessly turned and strode out back of the saloon, then led them in a group among the scattered, irregular little adobe one-room homes called *jacals*. Mostly, these residences had what was called a *ramada* over their fronts; it was simply two or three skinny posts set in the ground, slats placed from the roof outward towards the posts, then sage, or fronds, or even sometimes old blankets and scraps of canvas flung over the top to create a splotchy and humid shade.

Beeman halted, eventually, down where there were fewer *jacals*, eased his sixgun up and down once to loosen it in the holster, and licked his lips. Ahead of him two or three hundred feet was a *jacal* whose *ramada* had been carefully and artistically erected — no doubt by that doting *vaquero* back at the bar of The Trinity *cantina*. There was even a red geranium plant beside the doorless front opening.

Frank Hudson stepped up. "That it?" he asked, and when Beeman nodded Frank angled off to their right, heading on around back. At once young Bob peeled off to do the same from the left. They would ascertain whether a saddled horse was perhaps tied behind the residence, which would mean of course that Pat Potter was still inside.

Juan Turcio, Jubal and Jeff started straight for the door. Ted Withers would have accompanied them but Juan turned, motioning him back, so Ted looked around, saw a lone clump of chaparral, walked over and knelt beside it drawing his sixgun to cover the front of the house.

Several grandmothers out hanging laundry or gossiping, saw these obvious preparations for a killing, and dropped everything to whip excitedly indoors and scream at children who were playing in the dust to do the same. When the children were slow to obey, younger women sallied forward with switches and swung lustily driving astonished offspring inside. Within moments the area around Elena Gardea's *jacal* was emptied of people, and except for angry scolding coming through glassless windows, it was also quiet.

Not all adobe *jacals* had two doors. One doorway was ordinarily considered ample. What would be the reason for two doors when it only meant a man then had to watch both ways at night when the half-wild dogs — and local two legged thieves also — prowled the darkness?

Jubal was directly in front of the door where he could see inside, but it was dark in there. Both windows, one in the west wall, one in the east wall, had blankets hanging over them; that too was common. Blankets kept out heat. They also, of course, kept out prying sightseers.

Juan was on Jubal's left. Jeff was on his father's right. Turcio looked over and raised an eyebrow. Old Jubal's right hand was faintly crooked at the elbow, his fingers brushing the dark grip of his gun. He nodded and Juan called out in soft Spanish.

"*Señorita*; you have callers."

The house emptily threw back Juan's words in a musical, low echo. On Juan's left young Bob appeared, gun in hand. He shook his head which meant there was no horse around back. Juan relaxed slightly and called out one more time. After that he stepped ahead of Jubal and Jeff, whipped through the doorway and drew his weapon. A shriek of female fury sounded from the interior darkness and something came hurtling. Juan ducked. A commode pitcher smashed against the doorjamb. Jubal and Jeff lunged ahead too, heaving their rawboned bodies through the doorway.

The girl suddenly went silent. Evidently those drawn guns sobered her from what she'd evidently thought

104

initially had simply been some amorous intruder's early-morning visit. She asked in quick Spanish what they wanted. Frank Hudson and young Bob also crowded inside, and finally, the last man to come in was big Ted Withers, his badge evilly glittering.

"Pat Potter," said Jubal harshly, glaring fierce scorn at the thoroughly handsome, tall and voluptuous girl whom they could see well enough once their eyes became accustomed to the gloom.

"He isn't here," she said, and backed away from them. Her house was simply furnished with a low bed, a dresser, a large oval mirror — a genuine rarity and worth considerable money — an adobe oven made into the wall, and several rickety old chairs by an equally as unsteady old wooden trestle-table.

"Where is he," growled old Jubal, "and how long ago did he leave here?"

She shrugged at them, her pale, handsome face tightening a little up around the eyes with fear. They were men, but not at all the kind of men she was used to. They were killers on a hot scent.

"He left very early. Before the town was awake. I don't know where he went."

"You know," said Juan Turcio, his eyes sardonically smiling. "You know, and you'd better say. My friends here aren't men to play games with. They want Pat Potter. They'll slit your gullet too, if they decide to, for lying to them."

The tall girl's eyes flashed, she tossed her head. "I know where he went, and none of you can make me say."

Juan Turcio kept his little sardonic smile. "Of course you know, *querida*. And you're sure because the deputy town marshal is here no harm can come to you." Juan turned, stepped over and hooked an arm through Beeman's arm. "Let's step outside for a few minutes."

Beeman resisted. Juan dropped him a slow wink while their backs were to the girl. Beeman then said, "Sure enough," and stepped out through the doorway with the man from Libertad.

Young Bob bent slowly, fished out that two-edged boot-knife he carried and straightened back up. The girl's defiance disappeared. "I'll tell you," she said. "He went to the old mine."

Jeff made a motion for his brother to put up the knife. "What old mine," he asked. "Where is it?"

Troy Beeman appeared in the doorway. "I know where it is. It's one of those old Spanish mines where they had Indians do the diggin' for them years back." Beeman hesitated in the doorway gazing at the girl, then jerked his head at her. "Come on; you're goin' to get locked up until I get back to town."

She protested instantly. "Why? What have I done?"

"Nothing," replied the deputy pleasantly, "an' I aim to make sure you don't do nothin', too. Like gettin' some kid around town to high-tail it to the mine and warn Potter before we get up there. Now come along."

They took her back to the jailhouse with a clutch of big-eyed people watching this happen, then they went to the liverybarn for animals. Sam Salton chuckled. "I've done more damned saddlebacking in the past twenty-four hours than I've done in fifteen years before that," he told them.

They left town heading northeast, and once more, people watched them go. The Pierces and Frank Hudson were worn-out men consumed by a fire that showed latent in their sunken eyes. Turcio, Beeman, Ted Withers and Sam Salton, looked weary enough, but not so worn and saddle-warped as the men from Texas, even though they too showed signs of hard strain.

There was speculation in Castroville. Only a couple of men could shed any light on what was happening and one of them had not a word for anyone; he just sat and whittled and looked as bitter as oak gall. The other one of course was the Texas barman; he talked, and he deduced a fair amount of what was true. Not that he gave a personal damn that some feller was in trouble with the law, but it certainly helped his bar-business considerably.

They made good time on their fresh animals from the liverybarn but primarily they could do that because, after all the endless sequence of fiery days with a bleached-out pale sky overhead with nothing in it but that lemon-yellow sun, this day some clouds drifted in from the north and east. Behind them lay a hazy cold-front, possibly coming down across the frigid wastes of upper Canada across Montana, Wyoming, Colorado, and then, before the gulf-stream warm currents dissolved it over New Mexico as they invariably did, it was stealthily obscuring the brightness, turning the day pleasantly sufferable for those bunched-up horsemen being led along by Troy Beeman.

"This here old mine," he told them as they went along, "has a lot of tunnels runnin' off it. No one knows 'em all any more, an' since there've been rumours of Indians gettin' buried in there every now and then, no one's ever really made much effort to explore the thing. Over at Santa Rita at the old mission there's a parchment map of the mine. They say the Spaniards took several million dollars worth of gold out before the U.S. acquired New Mexico and run 'em out."

Jubal wanted to know how many entrances and exits this mine had. Beeman said as far as he knew it only had the one opening he was leading them to. Then he pointed where a low barranca stood dead ahead. "The mine's straight down the front of the cliff yonder. I'm goin' up atop that barranca so's he can't spot us in advance, and so, if he happens to be outside maybe cookin' or somethin', we can spot him before he can duck inside." As their horses began to labour slightly climbing the rear slope leading up to the cliff drop-off, Beeman said, "Frankly, if he gets inside there an' knows we're outside, I don't know just how we can force him out."

"No need to do that," said Frank Hudson. "Loosen a few ton of dirt in front of the entrance."

Beeman looked shocked. The others, accustomed to Frank's grisly proposals, said nothing. At least old Jubal and his youngest son showed grim approval of Frank's idea.

They reached the top of the barranca but halted back a quarter mile where some brush grew, left their horses tied and went forward carrying their carbines. Up to now they'd let Deputy Beeman be their leader. Now, though, that changed as old Jubal motioned for his kinsmen to fan out as they advanced. "Get strung out and keep down low; when you get close enough to see down there, get flat down and don't let him see you if he's down there."

Not just the Pierces joined this skirmish-line advance, they all did, eight armed men stalking an unsuspecting outlaw who'd spent a pleasant night and was now prepared to take his quiet ease. Jubal told Sam Salton, who was on his right, this was the way for a worthless man to die; thinking back to better things. Salton regarded the old man oddly for a moment, said nothing and kept slipping along.

They halted when Ted Withers signalled from farther down the top of their mesa. Ted made the Indian hand-talking sign of horse. At once they all got belly-down Jubal inched ahead over wind-smoothed stone until he could see. On his right Sam Salton made a low grunt. He too could see down to the slightly rolling, grassy land below. There was a hobbled horse grazing down there, switching his tail, hopping now and then towards clumps of cured buffalo grass. The animal was out perhaps six hundred feet from the sheer face of the cliff. The men atop their barranca could see the horse perfectly but they couldn't see straight down until they'd crawled still closer. It was a respectable distance down, from up there, about a hundred and fifty feet. Even when it was possible to look down and see rock tailings, bumped up where Indian labourers had dumped them a hundred years earlier, it was still difficult to see the shored-up square opening of the mine-shaft. The only way the strangers knew it was there was by those tailings, and by the way Troy Beeman pointed.

Pat Potter had to be inside the mine since he wasn't in view outside. It was warm enough for a man to seek the eternal coolness of the mine shaft, but it wasn't really hot because that high haze was moving steadily southward towards them, beginning to obscure the sun somewhat.

"Sleepin' in there," said Bob, when they'd all drawn back again — except Juan Turcio, who still lay with his head hanging over the cliff, watching down there. "Sleepin' like a fat old hog full of acorns. We can sneak down there."

Frank Hudson had a different approach. "Couple of us can ride down. He'll hear the noise and step out to look. The rest of us from up here can catch him square as he steps outside."

"Wait a minute," protested Deputy Beeman. "This isn't a damned execution squad."

"You're dead wrong," said Jeff. "That's exactly what it is, mister."

"By gawd not while I'm around," snapped Beeman, turning on rawboned big Jeff. "I don't give a damn what he's done, he gets his chance the same as anyone else."

110

Jubal lay a bemused gaze upon the deputy from Castroville. Bob and Jeff and Frank also gazed at him, saying nothing. Ted Withers looked at Sam Salton, who finally said, "He'll get his chance, Mister Beeman." To old Jubal Salton then said, "If he's here alone that means they've divided up the loot from the Spencer bank. Kill this one and we'll never know where he cached his cut. Mister Pierce; we've got to get him alive."

Jubal turned this over for a moment and grudgingly nodded. When young Bob turned angrily on his father old Jubal said, "Boys; without these men we wouldn't be here now. Without them we might not get the other three. I saw we take him alive — if he'll let us. We owe these men that much."

Salton and Ted Withers began nodding, Juan Turcio came back to them, drawn by the anger in their voices. "We can bait him out," Turcio said smoothly, "I can crawl over and take the hobbles off his horse. That'll bring him out on the run."

It was so simple the others gazed at Turcio, almost abashed. "That's how we'll do it," said Jubal, in a tone that encouraged no argument. Young Bob subsided, but his face still flamed red as they turned and went hiking back to their horses. The high haze was thickening steadily above them. A noticeable fresh coolness was in the dry, warm air. Somewhere overhead the sun stood close to its meridian.

CHAPTER
TWELVE

Getting down off the plateau was no problem. They could have made all the noise that many mounted men ordinarily would have made and whooped and hollered to boot without Pat Potter hearing them. But after they got down to the southerly terminus of the slope it became another matter altogether. From here on they didn't dare show themselves on horseback or Potter's grazing horse would see them and perhaps nicker, the way lonely and curious animals sometimes do at other animals.

They tied the animals, un-shipped their long-guns again, and stood a moment silently speculating. Turcio pointed out where the little low humps stood. Without saying anything he traced out his probable course utilizing those humps in the land to hide his appearance from the mouth of the mine-shaft, which was visible to them all, now.

"With some luck," said the tall lawman from Libertad, "I can keep plenty of those humps between me'n the mine opening. But if that damned horse spooks or heads back towards the mine, you fellers be ready to give me plenty of cover-fire."

Old Jubal, the lifelong saddle-horse-man, turned back from making a long-range analysis of the hobbled animal. "He'll be a quiet critter," he pronounced. "If you can get close enough so's he sees you without sensing that you're stalkin' him, you won't have any trouble."

Juan Turcio lay a wry look upon the older man but kept whatever thoughts he had to himself. He left his carbine with Ted Withers and started forward. Those little humps weren't more than three to four feet high. They might have been caused by miners hauling out rock tailings and dumping them, but if that were so it was no longer possible to be sure because dust and dirt had comgrew over them as well.

Troy Beeman nervously made a smoke and lit up as they all stood back from sight watching Juan Turcio's progress. Ted Withers made the remark that if anyone could accomplish this, it would be the man from Libertad. "Used to scout for the army when he was a kid, against Apaches and the Comanch'. He's a good man in a pinch like this."

"Seems to me," drawled old Jubal, with a somewhat different view of Juan Turcio, "he'd be a good man under any circumstances."

Sam Salton dropped to one knee, leaned upon his rifle and intently watched for Turcio to show, now and then, between the humps. He said, after Turcio had covered several hundred yards, that it would be hard on a man having to move all bent over like that for any great distance.

The sky got a milky look to it. The sun was entirely obscured, finally. There was a little roiled wind in the upper atmosphere which occasionally let loose a vagrant breeze down across the land. The day lost its overtone of heat rapidly and became almost as pleasantly cool as wintertime usually was upon this ageless desert. It was unusual enough for this time of year to inspire Troy Beeman to say he'd only seen this happen in mid-summer a couple of other times in all the years he'd spent in the border country.

"It'll help Turcio," observed Hudson, whose only interest was what they were doing and why they were doing it. "It might even get cold in that damned mine and drive Potter out."

That wasn't likely; it was spoken by a man who was letting hope override sound reason. Regardless of the exterior temperature summer or winter, inside the mountain the temperature would always remain constant.

Turcio had gotten among the last hummocks out there. Beyond, the hobbled horse grazed contentedly, totally unsuspecting. What helped immeasurably too was that when the wind blew now and then, it came always from the north, blowing the man-scent away from the horse.

Turcio could of course by now see the black, shored-up hole into the mountain where Pat Potter was. None of the others could see that opening except obliquely, but they didn't have to see it as well; their lives didn't depend upon seeing it.

114

Young Bob ripped out a breathless curse. The hobbled horse had just flung up its head, standing like a statue staring straight over where Juan Turcio had disappeared behind the last couple of humps. None of the others moved nor made a sound but they stiffened, their fingers closed tighter around gun stocks. The next ten or so minutes were going to make the difference one way or another.

For five of them Turcio lay flat. It was very doubtful that the horse could see him, but he'd either made a sound or the wind had perhaps betrayed him, because the horse stood perfectly still for those full five minutes, staring at the hump which hid Juan Turcio.

Fortunately, a horse's capacity for prolonged concentration is non-existent. The animal gave a little hop, half-turning, and dropped its head to resume eating. The seven armed possemen didn't relax. Now, the next move was up to Turcio. Now, he had to talk his way up to that animal.

They couldn't see him. All they could do was watch the horse, which was visible to them from the shoulders up to where he stood amid the low dunes. When he turned his head and looked low along the ground, they guessed Turcio had spoken to him in soft and reassuring manner.

Jubal whispered, "He'll make it. I was right about the animal. It's quiet-natured."

For a minute longer horse and hidden man eyed one another. The watchers saw Juan Turcio belly-crawl closer. The horse hopped once and turned. If Potter happened to be watching from the mine-shaft, he'd understand at once that his horse was studying something hiding behind the hummocks. Old Jubal and Sam Salton crept out and lay prone, facing northward along the cliff-face. Whatever Potter did now, unless he simply retreated deeper into his hideout, he would be at the mercy of the possemen.

The little vagrant breezes came gustily now, and no longer seemed to blow entirely from the north. It was as though a silent battle was in progress, invisible to the men who were out in it, the warm southerly atmosphere clashing with that milky cold front which had slipped through to get this far south before meeting fierce opposition.

Ted Withers said, "Damn!" The horse had shied a little leaving an open space for Juan Turcio to cross before he could get close again. Jubal and Sam Salton eased out their weapons ready to fire if Potter showed himself. Apparently, Turcio either thought he was far enough out to be reasonably safe if the outlaw should see him and fire, or else he was simply tired of trying stealth, perhaps because it was prolonging rather than expediting what he'd crawled that far to do. In either case, he got up onto one knee. They could all see his head and shoulders as he turned and ran a swift, probing look along the cliff-face from north to south. Then he stood up and started for the horse.

The animal was hobble-wise; it knew it couldn't escape so it didn't try. It simply turned entirely docile, let Turcio kneel to remove the hobbles. then it also stood while Juan fashioned a crude lead-rope from the hobbles and, keeping the animal's body between

116

himself and the mine-shaft, began leading the horse back towards the cliff-face.

"The damned fool," muttered young Bob. "All he's got to do is spook the the critter. Potter'll hear it runnin'."

Jeff said, "He aims to make dead certain of that."

Withers and Beeman were disapproving too, and showed it the way they moved their feet with nervous little shuffling gestures. There was reason for this concern. Unless Potter was asleep in there — and even then he'd be a light sleeper; all professional outlaws got that way if they lived long enough — he'd eventually hear something. He was bound to. Furthermore, closer to the mine-opening those little humps got smaller; too small in fact for a man to hide behind them unless he lay flat and curled his body.

Sam Salton suddenly got to his feet, hefted his long-barrelled rifle and jerked his head at Jubal. Those two started forward keeping close to the face of the cliff. Once, when his brother would have rushed ahead to join the older men, Jeff caught young Bob and hauled him back, growling at him as he did so.

Now, Juan Turcio was getting close enough to the shaft to set the loose horse free. He stopped when he saw Jubal and Sam Salton hastening closer to the opening and for a long moment watched their advance.

Withers, Beeman, Frank Hudson and the Pierce brothers eased around all together and walked farther out where they'd have uninterrupted sighting towards the mine-shaft. Sam Salton paused once, a hundred or so feet from the opening, and raised an arm to signal.

Juan Turcio set the horse free, slapped him smartly over the rump with the hobbles, then dove behind a hummock and drew in his long legs.

Sam and Jubal knelt, snugged back their carbines and waited. The horse ran towards the cliff-face until he was only a few yards from it, then he swerved and raced along parallel to it, head up, tail flying, obviously enjoying his run. When he got closer and saw the two kneeling riflemen he slammed down to a sliding halt, snorted and whirled to go racing eastward out across the open land.

For while nothing happened. Even when there was sudden visible movement in the mine-shaft opening, not everyone could discern it. Salton and Jubal did though, and Sam said, "Steady, steady; he's coming!"

The man who emerged from the mine-shaft was tall and lean and rumpled. He was hatless and had a cocked .45 in his right fist. At first he saw only his horse making off towards the east in a run. He allowed the sixgun to droop while he momentarily stood, staring eastward, no doubt thinking what any man would think when he saw his only security getting farther and farther away.

Then he swore and stepped completely out into the overcast, gusty afternoon, leathered his gun and glared after the diminishing horse. Sam Salton seemed not to be breathing at all. Jubal was like stone. They both were dusty and tan, making them blend perfectly. Potter stamped ahead a few more feet, angry to the soles of his boots, apparently, halted and with both hands on his hips, glared after the horse. Something made him turn.

118

That was when he saw Withers, Beeman, and the Pierce brothers standing farther off and slightly away from the shoulder of their barranca. Potter seemed momentarily stunned. He didn't sight Jubal and Sam Salton until Jubal spoke, scarcely raising his voice at all as he snugged back his carbine ready to shoot.

"Don't move! Stand right there and freeze!"

The outlaw's head jerked at the closeness of that grating, iron-like voice. He saw the rifle and the carbine trained dead on him. He had a second to decide and regardless of what his normal thoughts might have been, this wasn't a normal situation; he would live or die in the next breath. At that distance those two riflemen couldn't miss, nor did they look as though they would.

But he took a moment longer to arrive at his decision. He was a cool, brutal man who faced life head on. He had to now flip a figurative coin and decide whether there was any chance at all, if he drew and fired as he tried to spring back into the shelter of the mountain. The coin fell against his hopes, evidently. Potter lifted his right arm away from his holster and held it away.

Salton said, "Watch him, Jubal. I'll disarm him." Sam stood up, stepped sidewards and walked ahead. He kept his rifle held low in both hands ready to fire. He and Pat Potter took one another's measure over the decreasing made it less probable that Potter would ever get back inside the mine again. When Sam was close enough he halted. He had a close view of the hard, cruel visage of the outlaw. There was no sign of surrender in Potter's smoky eyes so Sam said, "Turn around and raise both your arms."

Potter sneered. "You afraid to try it face to face?" he asked.

Sam's finger squeezed a fraction tighter on the trigger of his rifle. "Shut your damned mouth and turn around!"

Potter turned. For a moment Salton didn't move in. Even when he did, he angled so as to approach from the near-side, where he had Potter's holster in sight all the time. Then he eased down the hammer of his rifle and swung overhand. He didn't attempt to disarm the outlaw at all.

The blow was hard and solid. Potter's legs sprung outwards. He dropped straight down and lay in an untidy heap. A trickle of blood broke through his mane of dark hair. Sam Salton ignored it, stepped over, plucked away the outlaw's weapon, then turned and beckoned. Jubal stood up and started forward. So did the others, much farther away.

Jubal grounded his Winchester and stonily stared at the unconscious man. "I'd wish him dead," he said softly, "except for your money, Captain."

"He may die yet," responded Salton, also considering the fierce, merciless face of the unconscious man, then turned away as the others came trotting up breathing hard.

CHAPTER
THIRTEEN

Inside the cave they found a bedroll, a Winchester carbine, a man's crumpled hat which had recently been serving as someone's pillow, and several tins of beans and fruit which lay discarded and empty. Evidently it was exactly as they'd all figured; Potter, after spending a long night down in town, had come out to this place to catch up on his sleep.

But they found no money except several hundred dollars in paper and gold in the unconscious outlaw's pockets. This troubled Withers and Salton but only passingly interested the others. Troy Beeman, for instance, was interested in knowing where there'd be a reward on Pat Potter. Juan Turcio viewed their captive as something evil and dangerous and therefore liable to extermination; it was the same way he'd have viewed a rabid wolf or a rattlesnake or one of the pus-gut Gila monsters who crawled over this same desert.

"We'll load all his stuff," said Troy Beeman. "Down here where it's hell to collect taxes from folks, we auction off saddles and guns — junk like that — to help defray the cost of bringin' in a circuit rider."

This made sense so they emptied the mine of all Potter's possessions, distributed them around, then brought over their horses to stand in the pleasant coolness, smoking, looking at their prisoner, and awaiting his return to consciousness.

"Maybe you hit him too hard," said Troy Beeman, slightly apprehensive about this.

Sam Salton was doubtful. "Not hard enough. That man's got a skull two inches thick." Sam bent, caught hold of the outlaw and heaved him up to his feet. It surprised them all, except Ted Withers who knew Salton. The reason it surprised them was that although Potter was a large-boned man, and therefore heavy, Salton raised him up one-handed. He also shook him. "If one of us had a canteen," he muttered, and shook the outlaw again.

It took a full fifteen minutes and by then that silent, invisible war in the heavens had been decided, as always, in favour of the gulf-stream air. The mistiness got diluted. The chilly little gusts of wind atrophied, and by the time Pat Potter groaned and opened his eyes, it was just beginning to turn warm again.

He raised a numb hand and felt the top of his head. There was a deep, ragged gash up there. His dark hair was matted with blood. The injury obviously was painful. Troy Beeman, showing no compassion, said, "You'll live. You're goin' to have a beauty of a headache for a day or two, but you'll live to hang, Potter."

Sam Salton still had hold of their prisoner by the shirt-front. He gave Potter a slight shake to catch his attention. "The money," he said. "Potter; whether you live or die right here depends on your answer. Where's the money you stole from the bank up at Spencer?"

122

The outlaw's eyes seemed to bother him. He braced both legs to stand without Salton holding him, but he put both hands across the upper part of his face. "What the hell'd you slug me for," he gasped. "I was quitting."

Salton shook the man again. "The money, Potter. Where is it?"

But their prisoner was too ill for answers right then. Troy Beeman led up his horse, got astride and kicked out his stirrup at the same time extending a hand. "Get up behind me," he said, making his abruptness carry to them all, not just to the outlaw. "We're goin' back to town."

Young Bob stepped between, facing Beeman. "Not so fast," he snarled. "You can take him back directly; right now we got some talking to do."

Beeman leaned down, his face reddening. "Get out of the way," he barked.

Jeff gave his brother a light shove. When Bob whirled big Jeff stonily looked at him. The younger man backed off, turning sullen and vengeful-looking. Sam Salton and Ted Withers led Potter over and heaved him up behind the deputy town marshal. Wordlessly, old Jubal had been observing all this. Now, he went across to the livery horse he'd ridden out here, wordlessly got astride and motioned for his kinsmen to do likewise. They all did, and to a knowledgeable observer it wouldn't have been feisty young Bob who'd have needed watching, it was Frank Hudson.

They got started, some carrying part of Potter's outfit, some packing his weapons. The sun was trying to burn through but didn't succeed. They got all the way back to Castroville to the jailhouse before it finally got clear of the gauzy little wisps of haze left behind by the vanquished cold-front.

They'd all forgotten the girl until they trooped into Beeman's building and she screamed imprecations at them in both Spanish and English. Among other things, she said she was starving. She also rattled off tumbling sentences at Potter, who was steady enough on his feet now to balefully regard her. She saw his menacing look and protested volubly that she hadn't betrayed him to the possemen. He didn't look as though he believed it and the possemen didn't look as though they were surprised at her for lying.

"I need a doctor," said the outlaw, glaring at his ring of captors, noticing their haggard, worn faces, their temptingly close-by holstered weapons, and finally, their faces, which were merciless towards him.

"You'll get one," said Frank Hudson. "But not for a scratch like that. I want you to tell me something, Potter; I want you to tell me why you killed my wife and her sister down in Deaf Smith County, in Texas."

Potter's eyes sprang wide open. He regarded Frank for an astonished moment, and as gradual realization came, he turned just enough to also stare at young Bob, at rawboned Jeff, and finally at old Jubal.

"You been on our trail since then?" he asked.

Frank said, "Don't act surprised, Potter. You aren't dumb enough to think you can do things like that and not have men hunt you down."

124

"I didn't do nothin'," exclaimed the captive. "I was down at the barn watchin' the horses. It was Slade — and the others."

Frank gently pressed his lips together. He was half a foot shorter than the outlaw but he happened to also be half again as broad. He said, "You're a damned liar, Potter. So was Riley." He started shuffling forward. Troy Beeman would have interfered except that Sam Salton caught his arm and drew him back. "You're going to end up like Riley too."

"Riley?" murmured the outlaw. "You sayin' Joe Riley's dead?"

Juan Turcio smiled. "He couldn't be anything else with all that lead in him, Potter. I'm the one who found him. These men riddled him — after he tried to waylay them."

Sam Salton released Troy Beeman. Sam asked again where the money was, but Potter was getting too many jolts one right after the other, to heed Salton at the moment. Ted Withers handed him another when he described in all its grisly detail the slaying of the man left in the bank up at Spencer. "That one was Jack Slade," Withers said. "There's not many of you left, Potter. Donland, Ames and Smith."

"Jack didn't get out of that lousy bank," groaned the outlaw, seeking a chair or bench to sink down upon. Jeff stepped over and kicked away a chair. Potter turned on him with a snarl. Jeff stood his ground.

"Go ahead", he said, leaning a little as though inviting Potter to strike him. But the outlaw drew back.

Salton never deviated despite what the others said or did. "The money, Potter," he said quietly. "Where is it?"

Troy Beeman stepped to the desk and picked up some keys. Over across the room in her cell the handsome Mexican girl was watching what was occurring outside. She seemed more fascinated by her lover's captors than she was by Potter's troubled and confused defiance.

Beeman flung back a steel door and stood by it as Sam Salton went to work on the prisoner again, this time with no distractions also being hurled at Potter.

"You've got one chance," exclaimed Sam. "And it's almighty thin, Potter. Tell us what you've done with the money."

"Me?" exclaimed their prisoner, looking for that chair again. "Me do with the money?" I didn't do *nothin'* with it. Why should I have it, damn it all?"

Young Bob started to shout at the outlaw. Sam Salton suddenly cut him off with a gesture and stood in front of Potter as though something had just come to him; something that excited him. He said, holding his voice down as always, "Where were you to meet for the division of that money, Potter? Be careful about your answer. Your life may depend upon it. Where were you supposed to meet the others after you got through over here in Castroville?"

Potter staggered to the chair, set it upright and dropped down on it. He rubbed his eyes, which were bloodshot and watering. "I need a doctor," he groaned again. "I likely got a cracked skull." He suddenly reared up and glared indignantly. "What good am I dead to you?"

"None at all," said Sam, boring in, still speaking in the relentlessly dogged tone he'd been using. "But you don't need a doctor for that bump on the head, Potter. You're going to need one in a minute, though, to prise a slug out of your guts. Where is that money from the Spencer bank? Potter; believe me about this; I'm running out of patience with you."

"I don't have no damned stinkin' bank money," muttered the badgered outlaw, and dropped his face into both hands. "My damned head's about to bust wide open. I want a sawbones."

Frank edged in from the opposite side from Sam Salton. He tapped Potter on the shoulder. When the outlaw, surprised at this personal contact, the first of such an encounter with his captors, raised his head, lowered his hands, Frank struck him across the bridge of the nose. Potter cried out and almost fell off the chair. Frank shuffled after him. Troy Beeman swore angrily and moved. Ted Withers caught and held him. When he swore, Ted just shook his head and held all the tighter.

Frank struck Potter again, this time in the mouth. The outlaw moaned and dropped to the floor. Neither of those blows had been adequate for such a collapse. The standing men all considered Potter with fresh expressions on their faces. They had all sized their prisoner up quite differently. Potter looked mean and brutal, but he also looked tough and courageous. Now, he was showing something altogether different; he was

127

showing cowardice. Even granting his head ached badly and that Frank's strike had split his lower lip, he was still acting poorly.

Sam Salton raised him up and eased him back onto the chair. "The money," crooned Sam, putting his face close. "Potter; the money from the Spencer bank — where is it? We came a mighty long way to get it. Either you'll tell us where it is, or we'll go after the others over at Daggett and wring it out of them."

Potter's wet eyes lifted. "Who told you they're in Daggett?" he croaked. "How did you find that —?"

"They money," crooned Sam, still holding his face inches away. "Just tell us where the money is."

Potter held a hand to his smashed mouth, stupidly gazed at the blood when he lowered the hand, and raised his eyes at once as Frank Hudson came shuffling towards him again.

Troy Beeman swore at Frank. "You hit that man one more time an' so help me I'll lock you up an' fling away the key. That man's my official prisoner. We don't abuse folks down here, Hudson. If you try it again — ."

"You talk too much, amigo," said big Ted Withers, restraining the deputy town marshal with hardly any effort at all. "They're only goin' to half kill him. They wouldn't finish him off because I wouldn't stand for that either. So let's you'n me just sort of relax back here and watch."

"When the marshal gets back," cried Troy Beeman. "He'll lock up the whole blessed bunch of — ."

"Naw," said Juan Turcio, turning from the waist towards Beeman. "Naw he won't. Your boss and I been mighty close friends for ten years, Mister Beeman. I know him better'n I know myself."

Frank raised his palm to slap again but Pat Potter shook his head, saying, "All right. All right, I'll tell you where the lousy money is."

Frank reluctantly lowered his hand. The others fastened their eyes upon Potter. There wasn't a sound in the jailhouse. Sam Salton straightened up to his full height, kept watching the prisoner, and crossed his arms.

"Mike's got it."

"Mike Donlan?" asked old Jubal.

"Yeah. Mike's got the money. We all figured to lie over here in Castroville last night. I didn't know Mike'd changed the plan until after I met this Mex girl and buttered her up. When I met 'em down at the liverybarn afterwards an' they told me they'd decided to head on out for Daggett, I told 'em to go on, that I'd catch up some time today. I told 'em I had somethin' goin' for me last night and didn't want to drop it just because they were gettin' edgy again."

"Go on," said Sam. "They rode away and you stayed with the girl."

"That's right. I was tired so I went up to this old mine she told me about when I tol' her I wasn't goin' to sleep in Castroville today. Then the dirty little whelp — she sold me out. You fellers snuck up — and that's the whole damned story."

"How long were the others going to hang out over at Daggett?" asked Ted Withers, loosening his grip on Troy Beeman.

"Today an' tonight; until I caught up."

Salton said, "Potter; how come you haven't divided up the bank loot yet?"

"How come?" demanded the outlaw, raising his battered face indignantly. "We haven't had a decent chance to stretch our legs under a table yet — that's how come. But Mike said we'd divvy up an' split up over at Daggett. He said if there'd been anyone after us from up around Spencer we'd have known about it by the time we got to Daggett."

Frank Hudson turned towards the door. Sam said, "Where are you going?"

"To get a horse," snapped Hudson, and reached for the door.

Old Jubal said, "Frank! Just a minute. This isn't any one-man war. We're all in it." He looked at Sam. "I don't think ridin' into Daggett with them watchin' is the right answer anyway."

Salton agreed with a curt nod. "We'll take the stage." He turned on Troy Beeman. "Keep Potter safe, deputy. If he's not here when we come back, you better not be here either." Then Sam jerked his head and led them all out of the jailhouse in a grim rush.

It was then the middle of the afternoon, with the sun fully shining again, rolling up its waves of saffron heat.

CHAPTER
FOURTEEN

The afternoon stage from Castroville to Daggett wouldn't leave for a half hour. They booked passage, hauled their saddlery back into the stage company's office again, dumped it there then went in search of food.

While they were eating Troy Beeman came in to say he'd locked Pat Potter into the cell next to Elena Gardea and these two who were so enamoured the night before, were now heaping all manner of imprecations upon one another, not to mention the most grisly threats.

Withers looked at Beeman. "You'll right glad to see this bunch leave, won't you, Deputy?"

Beeman was an honest man. "I've never seen anyone in our town since I been deputy, that I wanted to see out of our town so bad."

Juan Turcio said, "It's nice to know you're loved," and called for more black coffee.

The stage was late and young Bob fretted. "Suppose this Mike Donland decides to pull out without waitin' for Potter?"

"He'd have done it early this morning, if he had," opined Sam Salton shrewdly, "because that'd mean he was runnin' off with Potter's share of their loot. A man doing something like that would want an early start."

The stage arrived in town from the west. There was another delay while the four-horse hitch was changed, then the station-master signalled for the passengers to climb aboard. Besides the three Pierces, Frank Hudson and Ted Withers, there was also Juan Turcio and Sam Salton. That was a load for any six-passenger coach, but when the wiry young cowboy strolled out and also heaved his riding gear atop to be tied up there by the driver among the other saddles, the load became impossible. Jubal shook his head at the guard when that worthy came sauntering out, rifle held cross-ways, and critically examined things.

"You got one more passenger than we can squeeze inside," said old Jubal.

The guard shrugged. "Climb on top," he said to the youthful rangeman, "or wait 'til mornin' and catch the next coach."

The cowboy smiled. "On top it is," he said to young Bob, turned and went around behind to the boot and vaulted up. Young Bob jumped down and also walked around back.

"You'll need company up there," he said, and began climbing.

They were about the same age and somewhat the same build. If there was any noticeable difference it was in their temperaments. Young Bob was fiery, impatient, testy; the other youth was quicker to smile, more philosophical. They made a good pair together.

It made more room inside the coach too, for which the others were grateful, but even so, when the driver and guard climbed high to also take their places, the coach settled on its thorough-brace springs. Ted Withers called something to Troy Beeman, who stood upon the plank-walk. The deputy gravely inclined his head; whatever he thought of those strangers who'd come into his town causing turmoil, he showed no sorrow at all over their leaving.

The coach lurched once when the tugs snapped taut, then started ahead. Jubal, eyeing solemn Frank Hudson, told the others they'd have to come back to Castroville. He didn't say why they'd return and they didn't ask; they all knew. With the exception of Withers, Sam Salton, and less likely Juan Turcio, they didn't want Pat Potter tried, they wanted him dead.

Jeff eased back as best he could in the cramped quarters and watched the waning day speed past. It was typical of stagecoaches that they scuffed up a big billow of dust, ran hard for a mile or two beyond town because it looked romantic to break away in a big flourish, but once out on the road they slowed to a dull walk or a jarring trot. When this happened, now, Jeff shook his head. He had gauged the sun and now said he thought it would be dark by the time they reached the next town.

No one disputed him. Actually, Turcio, Salton and Withers didn't care, but then they weren't motivated by the same all-consuming fire as the men from Deaf Smith County were. Young Bob probably would have cursed a little when the coach slowed, had he been in with the others, but atop the coach amid the saddlery, even a slow lope or a steady trot seemed fast. Moreover, Bob was getting acquainted with the cowboy up there with him.

The land lost much of its greenness as they progressed. When the driver whipped up his hitch into a lope again, some miles farther along, the desert was closing in once more. Evidently the sub-surface flow from the Pajaro River didn't extent too many miles beyond Castroville.

There began to be rocks too; some as tall as a mounted man and thick enough to weigh tons. Clusters of them stood here and there, along with spidery little paloverde trees whose trunks were a startling green colour. Nopal, catclaw, sage, dozens of different varieties of underbrush took over the land making it seem uneven and multi-coloured while actually it was all more or less a bluish-grey, the colour of leached-out alkali.

Where they halted stood a stone trough at roadside. Here, the guard and driver climbed down to water their horses. Here too, the passengers alighted to stretch cramped legs, swing their arms and generally work out all the kinks. Usually at these places the men exchanged gossip with the coachmen, perhaps had a smoke together, then went on again. This time they fared even better. The driver had a pony of whiskey which he passed around. Everyone had one swallow then the little bottle was handed back, considerably depleted. The driver didn't mind. He assured them he had another one cached in the boot.

134

"Gets so damned dry down there around Daggett," he explained, "that just water won't cut the scorch out'n a man's pipes."

They left the stone trough while the sun still stood balanced upon the far-away rim of their world. It still hadn't gotten as hot as it normally would have been, due of course to that earlier disturbance, but now the sky was its usual pale, brassy blue.

For a mile they talked a little, inside the coach, and atop it young Bob and his new friend resumed their cordiality. It was obvious to the others, back at the stone trough when Bob and the young cowboy had climbed down, that the stranger had been told of the long vendetta which had brought the Pierces and Frank Hudson so far; he looked big-eyed at Jeff and Jubal and Frank. Of course it was no secret, although obviously Frank and the Pierces would just as soon not have had Marshal Withers and Sam Salton along at the end of their private vengeance trail, but since everyone now knew why the men from Deaf Smith County were over in New Mexico, why they'd just have to conclude their project more carefully, not changing their purpose at all — which was to kill their enemies — but to be infinitely more painstakingly wary about how they did it.

Jubal and Jeff privately figured to return to Castroville for Pat Potter. But neither of them mentioned a word of this, even to each other. Deliberate killers become the most secretive of men, and with the best reason, obviously.

Juan Turcio told Withers they'd be hitting Daggett just about dusk. Ted nodded, his head rolling drowsily.

135

He was abruptly jarred half off the seat as the driver hit the binder with his right boot and simultaneously hauled back on his lines. The coach didn't stop, momentum prevented that, but it bucked and skidded nearly dumping Ted Withers on the floor. He swore, wide awake in an instant, throwing out both hands to steady himself.

A gunshot sounded, then another. From above the coach two nearer guns fired back at once. The primary perquisite of youth was instantaneous reaction. Young Bob and his friend up there had unlimited visibility too; they'd apparently seen whoever had fired those first two shots and had let fly back at them.

Sam Salton and Juan Turcio reacted almost as rapidly as did Jeff Pierce and Frank Hudson. They shoved pistols out the open windows of their coach and strained to sight something. Another pair of shots came, then several more in a savage little volley. The gun-guard was in the fracas now, using his rifle. It made a decidedly different sound from the hand-guns of their attackers, but it only got off three rounds, then Juan and Jeff, on the right side, saw a body drop down from the driver's seat. It was the driver. After that the gun-guard caught for the lines before they fell in among the horses and had no further time to defend his coach.

Juan and Jeff eventually caught sight of shadowy movement off in the westerly desert where jumbled rocks and brush thickly flourished, and fired. Sam and Jubal and Frank tried to ease in on that side too, but there wasn't room.

The coach slowed. Their guard was hauling down his horses and riding the binder with his booted foot until the rear wheels skidded, setting a drag that even a six-horse hitch couldn't have hailed along very far.

The moment the coach stopped everyone piled out, firing off into that westerly desert and fanning out as they did so. The gun-guard looped his lines, grabbed up his rifle and sat up there high above where he had the best view, firing judiciously now and then.

"Where are they?" called Ted Withers.

The guard lowered his weapon for a second and pointed. "Yonder, scuttlin' off through the rocks and brush. Looks like maybe three or four of 'em."

Jubal was already advancing. He turned, flagging for the others to come along too. They made a ragged skirmish line and went carefully for several yards before the guard called out.

"They're pullin' out. They had horses tied out there. I can see 'em. They're a long half mile southward now and ridin' fast."

Sam Salton re-loaded where he stood, put up his pistol and waited for Jubal to come back, then Sam said, "Damned bushwhacking stage robbers."

"They got a gut-full," exclaimed Jubal, grimly satisfied.

When they broke back out of the undergrowth young Bob and the gun-guard were kneeling in shade on the near side of the coach. Until the others walked on over they had no idea anyone had been seriously hurt.

The driver was dead. He'd taken a slug as large as a man's thumb straight through the brisket. His heart

137

had been torn to pieces. He'd been dead, actually, before he hit the ground after being knocked off his box.

The other one was young Bob's friend, the youthful stranger who'd climbed atop the coach back at Castroville. Bob's face was grey to the hairline.

The guard found their dead driver's secreted second pony of rye and brought it forward. Bob got two good-sized swallows down the cowboy. He smiled at them, his head rolling back until it touched the hat that Bob had shoved under him.

"Feel real puny," he whispered up to them. But within moments the whiskey did its work; his eyes brightened, colour returned to his face, and in a stronger voice he said, "Where did they hit me?"

Old Jubal knelt; he'd gotten down on one knee beside an awful lot of dead and dying folks since he'd grown tall enough to carry weapons. He had a gentle way to him with them. He used it now, smiling a little through the lines and creases of his leathery face. "Boy," he said truthfully. "You took it through the chest on the left side." He refrained from saying the bullet hadn't come out. "Now you just grit your teeth a mite, and we'll lay you out inside the coach, then get along to Daggett where there's got to be a doctor."

The cowboy's flushed face began to clammily perspire. "This is a hell of a way to beat you fellers out'n your seats inside the coach, ain't it?" he said, and grinned at them.

They lifted him as gently as possible, got him inside, made him comfortable, then motioned for young Bob

138

to climb in with him. They told Jubal to also get inside. Salton pressed the dead driver's little flask into his hand.

Ted Withers said to the gun-guard, "You want to herd 'em, or shall I?"

"You know how?" asked the guard.

"Did it for a livin' fifteen years back."

"Then climb right up and he'p yourself, Marshal, because one thing I ain't particle of good at is herdin' along a four-horse hitch."

They put the dead driver in the luggage boot out back. They'd have lingered a while and gone looking for tracks, for something that might help them identify their attackers, except for that bad-off youth inside. As it was, they got back aboard, on top and three on the box, and started rolling again.

"Stick-up-men," opined the guard, then relaxed a little by bitterly cursing. "Whip Barrett was one of the best drivers I ever knew. Drank a little, but hell, as I told the boss, Whip Barrett drives better half loaded than anyone else drives stone sober."

"Does this happen often out here?" Jeff asked.

The gun-guard shook his head. "I been on this run seven months now, and it's never happened before. More'n likely they was some cowboys out of work who figured to take some cash off the passengers. We never carry no bullion or anythin' like that. And it surprised Charley as much as it did me when that first one jumped out wavin' his pistol at us, out there in the damned brush. I reckon it surprised Charley even more, for he forgot to hit the brakes until that feller fired. Then he stomped on the binder right hard. Them kids on the back shot back at that feller. The others opened up then, only we couldn't see 'em; they stayed low in the rocks and stuff."

Ted Withers was a powerful man. He had shoulders, arms and wrists of steel. He knew exactly when to exert a little pressure and when not to. As he drove along, he seemed to become absorbed in his chore of driving. Even when the town of Daggett appeared dead ahead in the gathering twilight, he didn't raise his head.

Inside the coach young Bob, leaning down, tilted his head. "Paw," he said. "His eyes ain't focusin'."

Jubal didn't look down. He said, "Son; the boy is dead. He never had a fightin' chance. That slug tore him up bad inside. He bled to death internally."

Bob's face acquired a stunned, incredulous expression. He stared at his father without even blinking, until finally he looked down at the quiet, grey face below him. Then he hid his face in his hands.

CHAPTER
FIFTEEN

Death never makes a sound. Old Jubal and all the men his age and older knew that. It might come in the fury and tumult of battle to touch this one, that one, another one, but when it reached for the man or men, they went silently. It was perhaps as much this total lack of anything at all that shook up young Bob so badly. But it undoubtedly was also the fact that he and the youthful rangerider had hit it off so well up atop the coach.

By the time Marshal Withers tooled the coach into Daggett at a steady fast walk, there were lights on in the saloons, most of the houses, up and down the main roadway, and there were two red lanterns hanging on hooks out front of the stage depot. That was customary. In this case it helped Withers select the building where he'd halt his outfit.

The town marshal at Daggett was a hawk-faced old man who had at one time been a bad man to cross, but who was now riding out his closing years in a back-wash town where ordinarily his reputation would have been enough. When the stage-line manager ran down to fetch him back, this big old shaggy individual viewed the two corpses laid out on the plankwalk in

141

front of the company office, showing nothing at all on his face except the grim acknowledgment that death had come.

The gun-guard started explaining while the other passengers worked at getting down their saddlery. A big crowd accumulated out of the thickening night the way flies gather over a carcass; without anyone actually telling them there'd been a tragedy, but by some mysterious instinct, knowing there had been.

The town marshal's name was Jack Hart. He peered at the Pierces, at Frank Hudson, at Juan Turcio, who nodded at him, and finally at Sam Salton and Ted Withers. He knew the latter pair, and slowly gave them a grave, dignified greeting. Then he said, "You heard the guard; is that how it happened?"

"Word for word," conceded Marshal Withers.

"Then I'd best get me up a posse," muttered the aged lawman. "Went westerly, you say, guard?"

"Southwest, Marshal. But that don't mean anythin'. They'd likely change course a dozen times if they figured someone'd be after 'em."

"They'd better figure that," growled the old man, looking at the dead men again. "Around Daggett anyone who gets on the wrong side of the law damned well better figure that."

The Pierces were studying Jack Hart. Juan Turcio turned and began pulling their carbines and Sam Salton's long-barrelled rifle out of the coach's interior. As he handed around their guns Daggett's lawman called for volunteers among the crowd of townsmen standing dumbly around. He got six men but the others

142

began drifting away. It was getting along in the evening; even to a greenhorn the obvious thing was that since they couldn't cut any sign in the dark, as possemen about all they could hope for was to stumble onto the outlaws, and in a country as big as this southerly desert that was a remote possibility, particularly since the outlaws would be watching and listening too.

Marshal Hart sent his six recruits after their mounts. He detailed several other men to hauling the corpses away. He then turned towards Ted Withers and said, "Well, Marshal; you sure as hell brought us trouble this time."

Ted's eyes drew out narrow. If he'd intended to answer back he didn't get the chance. Marshal Hart turned, pushed through what was left of the dwindling crowd and went stalking southward down towards his jailhouse. He patently wasn't happy about what he had to do.

Jubal said quietly to Sam Salton, all combing the westerly desert in the dark would accomplish, would be to mess up the tracks out there, and possibly scare the outlaws out of the country. Sam agreed, but he also said it was Marshal Hart's bailiwick, and although he was an old man now, there'd been a time when two-bit stage-robbers like that crew wouldn't have had a chance if Hart got on their trail, even in the dark.

Frank Hudson untied his filthy old jacket from behind the cantle of his saddle, shrugged into the thing and looked around at Daggett. It wasn't much of a town; it looked almost the same as Castroville except that it was perhaps a block longer and a block deeper.

There was a telegraph office across the road, two cafés instead of one, and a *cantina* which bore the decidedly Texas name of *The Longhorn*.

But Frank's mind wasn't on any of this, apparently, for he eased up between Sam and old Jubal and said, "Donlan and the others won't be around tonight."

Jubal looked down at his son-in-law, waiting for an explanation. He didn't get it because Sam Salton gave Frank a knowing little nod as he said, "They sure won't, at that."

"What you two talkin' about?" Jubal asked, a little annoyed.

"They hit our coach," said Salton. "Is that what you were gettin' at Mister Hudson?"

Frank nodded. "The guard said three or four. It'd be three, with Potter in jail over at Castroville."

Jubal lay a hand alongside his bristly cheek and thought. "If it was them," he eventually murmured. "It'd mean they wasn't figurin' on stayin' out the night over here the way Potter said."

"Potter was a fool," stated Frank. "He let the others ride off with his share — for that Messican tramp. The others'd feel about the same way, I reckon. They were probably already on their way when they spied our coach and figured to knock it over for whatever the passengers might be carrying."

"Son," said old Jubal wearily, "I hope you're wrong. I'd kind of figured on cornerin' them in one of these saloons, gettin' it all done with tonight, then rentin' me a bed at the roominghouse and sleepin' for a week."

144

They left their saddlery at the stage office despite the warning they elicited from the agitated manager that he always closed his office at seven o'clock sharp, and went in search of a café. They talked, too, as they did this. Only young Bob was indifferent, silent, and slouched.

When Marshal Hart went jogging grimly out of town with his posse they stood to watch him pass. There were reservations among them, but not a word was said.

Later, after they'd eaten, Sam Salton bought cigars and handed them around. Only Frank and young Bob declined; neither of them smoked. Outside with the soft night all around, they discussed their predicament. It wasn't at all certain the stage robbers had been Donlan, Smith and Ames. As Ted Withers said, "If Hart gets 'em — whoever they are — fine. But meanwhile it won't hurt a bit for us to spread around and see what we can learn."

Sam Salton paired off with Jubal. The others went in pairs or singly. Salton and old Jubal headed for the nearest saloon, on the way Sam said he thought they should keep an eye on young Bob. Jubal agreed. He said, "The boy's considerable like his maw was. Him an' my youngest girl. Their maw was a high-spirited woman, pretty as a summertime sunset, but powerful high-strung." Jubal puffed a moment on his stogie then removed it and said, "I tell you, Cap'n, the boy's lightnin'-fast with a gun. I sure-Lord never taught him. All I impressed on all my kids was live decent so's you can look folks square in the eye, take nothin' and give nothin' when it comes to trouble. But I never taught him to handle a gun. It's just natural to him — I'm afraid."

Sam stepped over the door of the saloon and looked past at the crowd inside. The room had four high-hung lamps with fresh-trimmed wicks and highly polished mantles. No Mexican owned this place. Even the floor had fresh sawdust down.

There were cowboys at the bar, smoke hazed the entire room, and around the outer wall were card tables, mostly occupied. When Jubal joined Salton in peering in out of the night, he didn't even know who he was looking for. That is, although he had three empty names, he had no physical shapes to flesh them out with.

"If Hart had stayed in town," mused Sam Salton, "he could probably identify most of those men in there for us. As it now stands any of them could be the bank robbers, or none of them could be. A hell of a good way to get killed would be to barge in there calling out names and looking like we were the law. This close to the Mex line half those men in there would have their reasons for shooting their way out."

Jubal stepped back quietly. "Let's go down to the liverybarn," he suggested. "One man who always has answers in a town is the liveryman."

They started southward through the warm night side by side. "You're going to kill them on sight," said Sam Salton, "and I don't exactly blame you, Jubal. But that's going to hand Ted Withers a mighty poor hand to play out."

"I didn't want him along, Cap'n. I didn't want any of you fellers along. We'll get 'em without no help. We've already done a fair piece of business with 'em."

Salton looked around. "Yeah. But next time don't expect someone to come along at the last minute and save your bacon like Juan Turcio did."

Jubal stopped, regarding Salton quietly. "You knew?"

"No, I didn't know, Jubal, but I'm an old hand at putting two and two together. Back there at the jailhouse when we were questioning Pat Potter, he gave me the clue that took us down here to Daggett. I knew, the minute he convinced me he didn't have any of the Spencer-bank-money, the others would be waiting somewhere close by for him, because if they hadn't divvied up then they also hadn't split up. The same in this place; whether those stage holdups were the men we want or some other men, my instincts tell me this is the place we'll run them down."

"About Juan Turcio," murmured old Jubal, bringing the topic back to where it had been before Sam had wandered away from it. "He told you what happened over at Libertad."

"Juan hasn't mentioned that killing at all, since he coloured it up enough to get you men out of the jail-house back in Spencer. He doesn't dare mention it. After all, Ted Withers happens to also be a deputy federal lawman. He can arrest the four of you here in Daggett just as easily as he could've done it back in Spencer. Turcio deliberately sprung you fellers. I can also tell you why, although I didn't know it at the time."

"Why, Cap'n?"

"Because Juan Turcio was out to kill Riley too. You men simply saved him the trouble, and perhaps you also saved his life as well. He'd be aware of that, Jubal. And Turcio would believe someone like Riley deserved exactly what he got, so Turcio would try to help Riley's killers."

"You know the reason, Cap'n?"

"Turcio's wife."

Jubal inclined his head. "You're pretty smart for not bein' any older'n you are, Cap'n. Now I got one question to ask: what you aim to do with all this information you got?"

Sam Salton's lips lifted a little, sardonically. He said, "Forget it, Jubal. I've already forgotten it. I don't pass judgment; who am I to say how other men have to live? Let's get down to the liverybarn."

"Wait. You figure to tell Withers?"

"No. Nor anyone else. Let's get along."

They resumed their way with a depth of silence between them. It was in Jubal's mind that a law-abiding man such as Sam Salton definitely was, would have a heap of wrestling to do with his conscience for hiding the identity of murderers. Perhaps more to the point would be the simple fact that Salton would have to carry his guilt by association all the rest of his life. It wouldn't be an easy thing to do for any man.

When they reached the liverybarn two men, both hostlers, were standing together in the centre of the run-way looking disgruntled and unhappy. At sight of Salton and Jubal Pierce they turned, wiped their resentful faces clean, and gravely nodded.

148

Sam said, just casually, "You boys look like a thief just made off with your best horse." He'd only intended to start the conversational ball rolling. He hadn't meant meant anything specific at all, but the oldest hostler, a beefy, paunchy individual in his fifties, dropped a thunderous scowl upon Salton and shot his bitter answer straight back.

"For a plumb stranger, mister, you hit the nail just about on the head. He wasn't one of our best horses, but he was plenty good."

Sam halted, owlishly regarded the beefy man a moment, then said, "Tonight; you mean someone really did steal a horse from out of this barn, tonight?"

"Yep. And Alf here could've shot him, too, if he'd had his damned gun on. On'y he didn't have, so like I been tellin' Alf, what in the name o' common sense is the point of ownin' a .45 if a man don't never wear it?"

"This thief," said Jubal, suddenly taking up the initiative. "What was his name, do you know?"

"No, mister, I don't know his name. Furthermore, we heard what happened to the evenin' stage, an' it wasn't one of them fellers either."

"How do you know that?" Jubal asked, and stood there hanging on the liveryman's reply.

"Because, mister, he didn't steal that danged horse until about a half hour back — an' that was a hell of a long time while after the robbery."

Jubal nodded. "What did he look like?"

"Young," said the other man gruffly. "Young'n sunburnt to a dark colour. Wore his weapon tied down. I'd say he warn't more'n nineteen years old. Moved

149

smooth as a big cat too. I seen him sneak in, swipe a saddle, blanket an' bridle and head for the stall with the buck-skin horse in it. But I didn't have m'gun handy, an' anyway, like I was sayin' just before you men walked in, I wouldn't have drawed on that young buck even if I'd had the gun on. I can spot the lightnin'-fast gunslingers a mile off."

"Wait a minute," broke in Sam Salton, who'd just seen the colour drain out of old Jubal's face. "This young feller — was he about as tall as I am with blue eyes, light hair, and clothes that were plenty stained and mussed?"

"That's him to a T, said Alf. "Say, mister; you two fellers wouldn't know him would you?"

Sam didn't answer. He and Jubal looked straight at one another. Old Jubal said, "Why; but why?"

"He'll be goin' after them too," replied Salton. "He'll want some skin off somebody for what they did to that young cowboy on the stage this evenin'."

"That's crazy," murmured Jubal.

Sam nodded. "You wait here. I'll get the others. We'd better find young Bob."

CHAPTER
SIXTEEN

But it wasn't that easy. For one thing the liverymen flatly refused to rent horses to Jubal and the others until they'd named the young cowboy who'd stolen their horse. Jubal dug out what remained of that sixty-six dollars they'd pooled when they'd ridden out of Texas. He offered to pay rent on the horse young Bob had taken, plus the horses they'd need now to go after him, and pay in advance.

That somewhat mollified the hostler called Alf, who didn't appear overly-bright at best, but the other nightman was less susceptible, although the sight of that crumpled wad of money made his eyes glow with slightly less malevolence and slightly more piqued curiosity.

"He's with you fellers, I take it," this man said, as Juan and Ted Withers came walking in out of the night. "Well; when Marshal Hart gets back he'll want to look into this. After all, the boy done took the horse and outfit 'thout so much as sayin' howdy-do. An', mister, that's horsetheft or I never heard tell of — ."

"Liveryman," boomed Ted Withers, frowning straight into the other man's eyes. "You're being offered fair pay. That keeps it from being horsestealin'."

"Yeah," bristled the hostler. "And who might you be, stranger?"

Ted fisted his deputy U.S. marshal's badge. The liveryman squinted, bent low and looked harder, then straightened up with his expression clear again. "If I'd known the lad was on official gov'ment business . . ." he muttered, and turned on Alf with a roar. "Don't just stand there, confound you Alf, go get horses saddled up for these here gentlemen!"

When they were ready to depart, were in fact mounting up near the lighted front doorway, a stocky man wearing a shoe-string tie and a black frock coat who was bareheaded and dark bearded, came hiking on up. "Whoa," he called commandingly, then moved closer to peer at the mounted men. "Marshal Hart told me just before he left town there's a stranger in town who's a federal deputy marshal. By any chance would one of you be that gentleman?"

Ted leaned upon his saddlehorn looking wry. "That's the second time in the last fifteen minutes I been called a gentleman, mister. I just might shuck my job up at Spencer and move down here to Daggett. I'm the federal deputy. Who are you?"

"Doctor Angus McPherson."

"All right, Doctor; I'm right proud to know you. Now what is it you want; we're in a kind of a hurry."

"I treated a wounded man an hour and more ago, Deputy. He'd been winged a grazing blow across the left shoulder, and again under the left arm alongside his ribs."

152

Frank Hudson fixed the medical practitioner with his dead-eyed stare. "Did you get his name, Doctor? Who was he?"

"I don't know. I didn't ask his name. But he had two friends with him who held their guns on me while I patched him up. Then the three of them rode off into the night northward. I went outside to get a better look." McPherson held up a hand. There was a large gold coin in it. "They tossed this down for my services."

Ted reached, took the coin and examined it closely. "So new it hasn't had time to tarnish. Sam; this came from the Spencer bank." Ted dropped the coin into his pocket. "Evidence," he told Angus McPherson. "You say they headed north?"

"North, Deputy, parallel to the roadway." Doctor McPherson paused, then said, "You'll find them. At least you'll find the one I patched up."

Sam Salton saw something in the medical man's face. "What did you do?" he asked.

"Put black pepper under the first course of gauze over both wounds. When the body fluids soak through and exertion causes the gauze to separate, that injured man will be in real torment. Riding will only aggravate it. I think, as wrung out and dissipated as he was, that one'll throw in the sponge after a couple of hours."

Frank turned to Jubal. "What about young Bob?"

"Leave him be," replied the older man. "He'll be ridin' southwest more'n likely. We know now Donland, Ames and Smith didn't head that way. They hid out until dark to get one of them cared for by the doctor

153

here, then they lit out northward. Bob'll get exactly what he deserves — a night-long ride to cool him off."

Jubal nodded stiffly at the medical man, reined on out into the roadway and set his livery animal to a choppy little trot. The others strung out behind him leaving both liverymen and Doctor McPherson standing back there in the lighted doorway.

"I'll make a wager with you two," said McPherson to the liverybarn nightmen. "I'll lay you twenty to one when those men return they'll have dead men slung across their saddles. I don't know what it's all about, but I certainly know men dead set on killing when I see them."

The hostlers declined the bet.

Daggett had music in one of its saloons. The dark roadway was relieved by little pools of speckled lamplight here and there. A few men stood about in the pleasant night smoking and talking. When Jubal led his band of armed men past, looking neither right nor left but heading straight up the northward roadway, conversations dwindled and sober eyes followed the horsemen right up into the full darkness beyond town, and there lost them as they booted their animals over into a lope and headed arrow-straight up the roadway.

Sam told Jubal it was a lead-pipe cinch the outlaws hadn't kept heading north. They'd figure someone back in Daggett would have watched them ride out. Jubal nodded. He'd evidently already considered this. But there was something else, he told them all. "If that hurt one gets to painin' too much, they'd leave him up here some place. Now what we got to figure out is — just

154

how far could he go — then we got to spread out with lots of range between the lot of us, and commence searchin' for a wounded man or a tied horse."

That's what they did as they entered their second mile, fanned out so far they could just barely make out one another, and beat onward through the night looking for a man, a horse, or anything at all which might give them a hint.

Six miles out they came upon a camp of Mexican faggot-gatherers. These were elderly men; too old to hire out as *vaqueros*, which left them only this menial type work if they wished to survive. There were five of them with nine burros. Their bundles of sticks were neatly stacked, and the men were enjoying a game of Pedro on an old blanket next to their fire, but the second they detected riders around them, those five old men scattered out into the darkness like startled quail.

Jubal halted just beyond the fire and called to them in Texas-Spanish. "*Hombres*; this is a friend. I mean no harm. I want to know — have there been three horsemen ride past this place tonight?"

Two of the old men came back until they were barely visible on the far fringe of their firelight. "*Si, amigo*," one of them called back. "Three *vaqueros* riding fast. One was drunk and reeled on his saddle. You must know, friend, that we hadn't yet started our fire and therefore they failed to detect us in this formidable darkness. We watched and let them go, which was of course very natural since we are poor old men unable to defend ourselves."

155

Jubal threw back his head and howled like a wolf. The pair of Mexicans fled out into the desert again. Jubal then dismounted and stood beside his horse waiting for the others. They came, having relayed the call to the farthest man, which happened to be Ted Withers. When he appeared and out in the shielding night the faggotgatherers caught reflected firelight off Ted's badge, they timidly came forward again. This time all five of them. They didn't spy Juan Turcio right away, but when he called out in an amused way to them in flawless Spanish, chiding them for acting like old women, they moved right on back to their fire again seeking the one man among these hard-faced strangers who could joke in perfect Spanish at this bad moment.

Juan inquired again, asking pretty much the same questions old Jubal had asked, only in Spanish. He got back five simultaneous, prolonged and very flowery replies. Juan laughed. "Marshal," he said to Ted. "These men have just cinched it for us. They say that on northward in the direction the outlaws are riding is an abandoned goat ranch. That's the only decent water for thirty miles in all directions from here. That's where our men are heading sure as night follows day."

Withers nodded towards the faggot-gatherers. Then, on the spur of the moment, he fished out the gold piece he'd taken from Doctor McPherson and tossed it at the feet of a villainous looking old Mexican with a big droopy Longhorn moustache.

"For lousy *gringos* we pay pretty good, eh?" he said.

The old men watched their companion stoop, retrieve the gold coin, bite it, hold it to the firelight,

156

then expand his burnt-black old leathery countenance into a grin that threatened to split the hide wide open. "*Caballeros*," exclaimed this old man. "*Gente de razon!*" He handed the coin to one of the others so they could all examine its astonishing worth. "*Mucho caballeros, señores. Mil caballeros!*"

Juan Turcio swung back astride laughing. "You take care, old ones," he told them in Spanish. "Pulque and tequila are hard on old arteries."

Jubal didn't smile. Neither did Jeff or Frank Hudson. Frank never smiled anyway. Sam Salton was quietly amused but he said nothing until they were heading back towards the roadway and he happened to fall in beside Ted Withers. Then he said, "That makes the third time someone called you a gentlemen. Only this time you were a great, a grand gentleman." Ted nodded, pleased. "But I doubt like hell if Doctor Angus McPherson, who looked to be a hard man to beat out of fifty dollars, will think so when we ride back to Daggett, Marshal Withers."

They found the road easily. The moon was up, thicker again than it had been the night before. There were stars tonight too, which also helped. The previous night there had been that milky disturbance in the upper atmosphere which had obscured all starshine.

The road ran northeast; it began digressing from its due-north course shortly after they left the vicinity of the faggot-gatherers. As soon as he began noticing the alteration in their course Jeff speculated aloud on this goat ranch up ahead. "The question," he said, "is whether these outlaws know the place is there or not. If

157

not, they damned well might ride right on past it in the dark."

Juan was less pessimistic. "They're kind usually makes it a point to know where things like waterholes are in this desert country. But whether they're up ahead or not, we're sure a hell of a lot closer to them tonight than we've been before."

"We'll find them," muttered Frank, pulling his hat forward. "What I'd like to know is where Bob went."

"We'll find him too," said Sam Salton. "Maybe it's a good thing he's wandering around on the southward desert. Less chance of him gettin' shot that way."

While Salton had been speaking the others gradually saw a light ahead and to their right. It was so insignificant at first it seemed to be little more than the steady glow of a firefly. By the time Sam spoke, though, it showed as a definite, man-made illumination of some kind, either a campfire — in which case it was a lot farther off than it seemed, to be that small — or else it was a lamp.

They halted, closed up a little and speculated. Frank said it was a camp-fire. Ted Withers chose to believe it was a lantern. Jubal wasn't too concerned. What he said was, "Jeff; you'n Frank scout it up. The rest of us'll wait here. And Jeff; take heed, boy. If it's them we don't want 'em spooked."

Jeff and Frank Hudson walked their horses away, striking out across the desert where night-shadows soon engulfed them both. The others dismounted to rest their horses's backs, made smokes and considered this odd phenomena. Sam Salton had reservations; as he saw it, even though it was reasonably late at night and no doubt most of the furor over the stage-robbery had atrophied back in Daggett, prudent and experienced outlaws wouldn't deliberately light a camp-fire this close to a travelled road and a town.

The others were less willing to attribute that much wariness to the men they were after. "Whiskey," stated old Jubal, "makes men do careless things. Whiskey and too much success. I reckon that'll be them up there all right. I'm sure hopin' it is."

The waiting was protracted. Even their horses became impatient after enough time had passed without Frank nor Jeff returning. Juan told Ted Withers if they didn't return soon he would go see where they were.

Then they came back, each man leading his horse and stepping carefully even when there was no longer any need for it. Jubal scarcely gave them time to get back up close. "Well," he called softly, "who is it?"

"It's them," responded big Jeff. "But they're at a camp of other men. Freighters heading south with two big wagons."

"How many, son?"

"The murderers are there, all three of them. They were washing out the wounds of that man the doctor put pepper on. He was cursing for all he was worth."

"How many of the others, boy?" Jubal inquired a trifle impatiently.

"Five that we lay out on the desert and counted. I reckon that's a driver and swamper on each wagon, and maybe a scout. The thing that's botherin' Frank and me, Paw, is how do we get those murderers away from the freighters? If we make a fight of it the way things stand now, some men'll get hurt who have no business in this at all."

Jubal cut across a suggestion Sam Salton was about to make. "Son; I figure the first thing we got to do is set 'em afoot. After that, we'll get 'em away from the others without too much trouble. Outlaws hate losin' mounts worse'n freighters hate losin' teams. You take away an outlaw's horse an' you've chained him to the ground where anyone can run him down."

Juan shrugged. "It'll work, providin' we can get to the animals. Providing they're not tied to wheels or somethin' at the camp."

"They're hobbled," said Frank. "But they're stayin' fairly close by. It'll be almighty risky. A sight riskier than back at the mine-shaft where there was only one gun, Juan."

"How far ahead?" asked Sam.

"Mile," replied Jeff. "All the same we'd best leave our horses right here. There's a lot of loose shale between here and there. All of us ridin' up there — they'd hear."

CHAPTER
SEVENTEEN

The freighter-camp was out back of the ramshackle old building which the faggot-gatherers had designated as the goat ranch. Even in watery moonlight it wasn't difficult to see why whoever had originally resided in that desolate place had pastured goats instead of perhaps cattle, sheep or horses. Nothing but a goat could have eked out an existence.

Except for the lack of rocks, this desert country northeast of Daggett was scrubby, sandy, and utterly worthless for anything. It was probable that even the unknown goat rancher had starved out.

There was a broad belt of shale which ran east and west. Sam Salton and old Jubal, striding along out front, encountered it first; pieces of flint-like stone wafers atop one another for perhaps a hundred yards. Sam turned to softly ask Frank and Jeff how far westerly it ran; whether or not by going over in that direction they might not get around it. Neither Jeff nor his brother-in-law knew. They said they'd crossed it by taking plenty of time, which was what had made their return so protracted. Frank then gestured for the others to follow him and started gingerly through. He hoisted all his weight onto one foot and used the suspended foot to feel for another place where the shale would support his weight without making its little brittle sounds.

The problem was of course multiplied. Earlier, there had been only Frank and Jeff. Now there was Jubal, Sam, Juan Turcio, and Ted Withers as well. Of them all Ted was the least dainty at gliding forward, so they put him in the rear and hoped that between Ted's caution and the fact that the others had previously trod down the shale he'd cross over, there wouldn't be noise from the rear of their line.

There wasn't. They got across the shale-bed without difficulty and halted where the sandy loam commenced again. Ted was profusely perspiring. He would have said something but by now they were close enough to see the little fire quite clearly. Sam and Jubal quietly conferred while the others loosened from the tension they'd felt while getting over the shale-rock. Sam's idea was to surround the camp if that was feasible, and send just one man in to spook the horses. Jubal was favourable except that he thought his son should go with Juan Turcio to run off the horses.

Sam gave in, at the same time pointing out that they wouldn't have any way of protecting one another if they spread themselves too thin. Jubal's practical reply was simple.

"It's goin' to be a fight, Sir. There's no two ways about that. My notion is to get their horses, then call over for the freighters to get clear. They're goin' to suspect someone — redskins or professional horsethieves of some kind — went after their animals. We couldn't

walk upon 'em nohow, after that, so it'll be a fight."
Jubal pointed. "We can get into prone positions on all
sides. The darkness an' the underbrush'll he'p us to
keep 'em in their fire-circle." He dropped his hand and
looked at Sam Salton, waiting. Sam nodded; whether
he entirely agreed or not, Jubal's practical observations
had been adequately sound. He turned. "Juan; you and
Jeff Pierce want to make a try for the horses?"

"Let me go with Jeff," said Frank Hudson swiftly,
giving Turcio no chance to answer. "We know the lay of
the land up there, Marshal Turcio don't."

Sam and Juan exchanged a look. Turcio shrugged.
Old Jubal stood looking at his son-in-law, his
weathered, dark old features softly apprehensive. But he
nodded, finally, offering Jeff and Frank an un-needed
warning. They immediately started forward, drifting off
to the left of the others, which was westerly. That in
itself indicated that they knew what they were about,
knew how the land lay up here.

Jubal canted his head to study the silvery moon,
three-quarters full. It was getting along towards eleven
o'clock.

Juan said, "I wouldn't want to be in the boots of
those freighters. It'd be like trying to sleep in a den of
rattle-snakes."

Jubal turned to studying that little fire on ahead. It
appeared to be dying somewhat, as though perhaps the
men up there weren't feeding it any longer. He
murmured, more to himself than to the others, "If there
was a decent chance we could maybe sneak up on
them. Most of 'em'd be asleep."

Sam Salton scotched that. "There's no chance of that. They'll have at least one man on guard." Sam also said, "Jeff and Frank should be getting into position now. The rest of us better spread out and do the same. Ted; you stay here on the south end. Juan; you head on around to the north. Jubal and I'll take the east and west. No shooting unless someone makes a run at you. Like Jubal said; we'll try and talk the freighters out of that camp first."

"Not a chance," muttered Juan Turcio, standing very erect and watching the distant firelight. "The others'll use 'em for hostages at the first sign of trouble. When those outlaws get set on foot, they're goin' to know . . ."

Old Jubal was inflexible. "Then they'll have to take their chances. The hell of it, not knowin' those outlaws by sight can complicate things."

That was an understatement and the others seemed to think so; Sam Salton said he wasn't going to fire on anyone unless he was positive it was one of the wanted men. Juan Turcio didn't go that far, but he shook his head in strong disapproval at old Jubal. Ted Withers cleared his throat and stood troubled.

"I don't know how we can separate 'em," he mumbled. "I had the finish of this pictured different. Now it's a damned lousy mess."

Jubal appeared unmoved. "Let's go," he urged. "The boys'll be after the horses soon now."

Jubal headed off towards the east. Sam Salton, watching him walk away, started to speak, changed his mind and walked away towards the west. At once Juan Turcio lifted the carbine he'd been leaning upon and also strode off through the quiet, soft-lighted, warm night. That left Ted Withers standing there barring the westerly exodus should the outlaws attempt to flee. Ted was morose and with good cause. Killing innocent men who through no choice of their own happened to be in the midst of a deadly surround wouldn't have appealed to very many men.

For a long while the night seemed endlessly motionless; seemed not to advance an hour or a minute. The stars serenely shown, that lop-sided old moon hung up there, fat and ungainly looking, and there wasn't a sound. That small beacon on ahead was definitely dying now. It was getting along towards midnight. To the men creeping into their surrounding positions on all sides, it seemed hours, ages, since Jeff and Frank had slipped forward. The worst aspect of any fight is always the waiting; it gnaws at a man's vitals. It plays like steel talons along the wetness of his nerves. It conjures in his mind all the disasters which can occur. In daylight it is bad enough, but after dark it multiplies as the minutes drag past, for there is in even the bravest men the ancient knowledge that the night does not belong to them; that it belongs to shapeless things and primeval fantasies.

A horse nickered. The men out on the desert who had advanced in, closing their surround somewhat, could discern two huge, wide-wheeled freight outfits, their side-boards five feet high, their running-gear clearly exposed beneath high wheels. That nickering horse set every nerve on edge; neither outlaws nor freighters slept so soundly a horse's noise wouldn't startle them out of a light slumber. For ten or twenty seconds afterwards there wasn't a solitary sound, then the horse nickered a second time, but after that the easily discernible drumroll echoes of loose horses on the move brought the silence and gloomy darkness to a crisis point. Jeff and Frank had been successful; now the renegades and freighters both, would come boiling up off their blankets, the freights to unsuspectingly curse a misfortune, the outlaws to whip this way and that believing it was no accident; believing there were men out there in the night hunting them.

Someone called triumphantly, "I got one. Damn it all, I roped one of 'em!" This man was heading straight towards Ted Withers when he shouted. Ted could hear the horse coming but until the man cried out he had no idea the horse wasn't running free.

For perhaps four hundred feet the horse's momentum dragged the swearing, stumbling man who'd roped the animal, along. The man refused to let go. He was heavy and thick-through. When his stubborn resistance persisted, the horse broke its stride, slackened its speed, was on the verge of giving up. It caught Ted's scent when only about a hundred feet away, and stopped very suddenly then violently shied to the left. That's when Marshal Withers got a good view of the burly man in the torn and rumpled, checked shirt on the end of that thirty-foot, seven-sixteenths catch-rope.

The man didn't see Ted right away. He was too occupied with the horse to which he was hanging with grim tenacity. With one horse, the freighters and outlaws could mount one rider who in turn could

166

locate the other animals and haze them back towards the camp again.

Ted rose up off the desert, poked his carbine towards the swearing man, who was now taking up his slack in right-hand coils as he profanely advanced upon the horse, and got within fifty feet before the burly man happened to twist his face away from the bewildered horse. Then he saw Ted and stopped like stone in his tracks.

"Not a sound," warned the deputy U.S. lawman, walked in close enough to see the wide garrison belt, the flatheeled, high-topped boots, and let his carbine barrel sag a little. "You with those wagons up there?"

The man gazed from big Ted's rugged countenance to his badge, then back to his face again. "An' who the hell are you?" he snarled.

"You got eyes," retorted the lawman. "Or did you figure I was born with this badge stuck to my hide!"

The freighter began slowly coiling his rope again. He looked around then back again. "All right; you got a marshal's badge. Sure I'm with them wagons; what'd you think?"

"One more smart-alec answer," said Withers, losing his grip of his patience, "and I'll teach you the manners your mammy forgot to learn you. Now keep your voice down. Are there three men up there in the camp with you — one of 'em with a bandage over his ribs an' another one over his shoulder?"

"There were," said the freighter, sizing up Ted Withers. "As for teachin' me manners, mister — just you set down them guns an' we'll see who teaches who."

Ted strolled closer, sized up the freighter, saw the man's powerful, sloping shoulders, thick torso and oaken limbs, then let his breath out quietly. "Some other time, mister. Right now we want those outlaws up there in your camp."

The freighter blinked. "Outlaws? Them's cowboys who work hereabouts. The hurt one's been down to Daggett to get patched up after a horse fell an' rolled on him."

"That hurt one," corrected Ted Withers, "was winged twice this afternoon above Daggett when him and his friends tried to hold up a coach I and some other fellers was ridin' in. No horse rolled on him — those wounds were made by bullets. Now walk on over close to me, mister, and turn around."

"Oh no you don't," said the freighter at once, drawing himself up to resist. "You don't crack me over the head, Marshal."

Ted pondered. He didn't like this man; he didn't even know his name or where he was from, where he was going, what sort of person he might be. And furthermore he didn't care. He had a violent private antipathy for the freighter. At the moment that was uppermost in his mind. "Mister; you either do as I say or get yourself shot, an' I don't have all night to wait on your decision either."

The freighter had evidently been thinking too, for he said, "Marshal; there are five of us with them wagons. You're not goin' to sneak up on the others like you done on me. There are also those cowboys you claim are outlaws. You aren't goin' to catch them nappin' either."

"What the hell are you tryin' to say?" snapped Withers, inching closer, poised to lash out with his carbine barrel.

"I'm sayin' if you prove to me you're not just some feller wearin' a badge so's you can even up some score with them cowboys, I think I can get the other freight-men to walk down here where we're standin', and that might give you a run on the cowboys."

Ted's attitude slowly changed. He still didn't like this burly man, but there was definite merit in what the freighter suggested. He eased off the hammer of his carbine, grounded the thing, drew forth his wallet and tossed it over. "You look at the identification cards in there," he snarled. "If that don't convince you, mister, then you're just not convincable."

The freighter examined Ted's wallet and its contents thoroughly, he nodded and tossed the wallet back. "I reckon you're genuine," he said. "All right; I'll call to my friends and we'll see what happens."

It didn't work out that way. As the freighter turned, cupping both hands over his mouth, a quick, slashing burst of gunfire broke out west of the wagons. It was a lethal exchange between two men back beyond the dying fire and another two men opposite them closer to one of the big wagons. For ten seconds the gunshots lanced the night with bluish flames and made deadly echoes bounce back and forth in the night. Then the firing stopped as suddenly as it had begun as each side sidled left or right to get clear of their old positions and seek new ones.

The freighter stood with his hands still cupped. He was astonished. Ted wasn't. He'd jumped a little when the first shots erupted, but Ted Withers was an old hand at this sort of thing; he seized the advantage, stepped over and hit the freighter hard across the top of the skull. The man tried to twist away at the last second, and only succeeded in looking into Ted's face, then he fell in a rumpled heap and the horse he'd caught, startled by Ted's sudden, swift movements, broke away with the lassrope around its neck and went flinging off westerly. Ted didn't even glance around to see which direction the horse took.

A man's voice up by the wagons called out a dull-sounding steady stream of curses. He sounded as though he'd been hit hard and was reacting typically to pain and surprise and hopelessness.

170

CHAPTER
EIGHTEEN

Sam Salton cried loudly over the noise and bedlam as three guns sporadically fired from around the wagons, telling the freighters to get clear, warning them that the law had their camp surrounded and wanted only those three outlaws over there.

Jubal called out too, his voice harsh and booming with the sound of Judgment Day as he told the renegades who he was, who the men with him were, and why they were going to kill the outlaws.

Finally, those three guns over near the camp went silent. Someone crept over and covered the fire with dirt. After that the only light came from above.

Gunfire became infrequent. The men who'd come to Daggett from up at Spencer began closing in, began inching forward so there'd be no chance for the outlaws to escape. That cursing man's voice trailed off into silence. When, during one of the little unpredictable lulls a deathly silence ensued, Ted Withers said loudly. "You freight-men up there. This is U.S. Deputy Marshal Ted Withers from up at Spencer. You fellers don't get mixed up in this. Don't offer no help either or you'll be accessories."

A slashing gunshot came southward probing the night for Ted. It came close, too, but this was a big country and flat, a man's voice bounced around in it like a rubber ball; the outlaw hadn't been sure where Ted had shouted from.

Off in the north Juan Turcio seemed to have approached the freighter-camp closer than his companions; when he cut loose he wasn't using his carbine as were the others, Juan fired off five fast rounds, ground-sluicing under the wagons, then he fell silent to re-load and the outlaws opened up towards the north with a vicious return-fire.

The freighters weren't fighting. Ted's fear that the renegades might use them as hostages wasn't coming to pass, and probably for an excellent reason; the outlaws had been caught too suddenly, too savagely, to try and make any moves except purely defensive ones. What might happen if the pressure slackened off was anyone's guess, but for the moment both attackers and attacked were fighting a violent battle for life with no time out for anything else.

Salton finally seemed to decide he was facing only his enemies; heretofore he hadn't done much more than exhort the freighters to get clear. Now, when someone fired up into the darkness where Juan Turcio lay, Sam snapped off a pair of fast shots at the outlaw's muzzleblast. A man sharply yelled over there, either hit or nearly so, and three guns whirled to throw lead easterly. Sam didn't fire back. For a while this worried the others. When a man stopped firing at the height of a battle he usually was knocked out.

Jubal, farther off in the west, suddenly detected the oncoming charge of a party of riders. He fired, raised up to listen, fired again to keep the pressure on the outlaws, then finally rolled to a new position and sat up, looking over his shoulder. The only riders besides themselves anyone knew about in the late night was Town Marshal Hart and his posse. If that's who was coming, then evidently they'd been drawn by the ringing sounds of a battle northeast of town.

Jubal dropped low again and called out: "Jeff; Frank; close in. All of you close in." Clearly old Jubal wanted this finished for all time before the possemen came up to tip the scale so hopelessly against the outlaws they'd surrender. He didn't want any more survivors like Pat Potter back at the Castroville jail. He edged forward too. So did the others, although they weren't as vengeance-minded. In particular, Ted Withers and Sam Salton wanted someone left alive up there. Three dead outlaws just might mean no one would ever discover where the money from the Spencer bank was cached. Potter hadn't known, so he was worthless. The man named Mike Donlan, leader, or at least unofficial chieftain of these killers and thieves, would certainly know, but since none of his attackers knew which gun belonged to Donlan, they couldn't spare the man when they returned the suddenly intensified fire from over by the wagons.

It seemed the outlaws were each firing two guns. They were; a pistol in one hand, a carbine in the other. Donlan had also heard that swarm of riders coming. All he and Ames and Smith had to know was that these were not friends; anyone else would be their enemy.

They called back and forth, making ready to run for it. Jubal yelled to his companions; he knew what was coming. But so did the others. There were no novices in this roaring battle. If young Bob had been there he'd have been the only man among them all who hadn't been in other fierce fights before.

One of the outlaws roared defiance and ran straight west. It seemed an incredibly stupid thing to do. Not because tough old Jubal was out there, but because that was also the direction of those oncoming horsemen. But it wasn't stupid as it initially appeared to be. Win, lose, or draw, the only chance those outlaws had of getting out of this alive was to get mounted. They couldn't even hope to escape on foot in the desert. It was a variety of madness for them to charge straight towards the greatest concentration of foemen, but the only alternative was to be picked off one at a time by the surrounding gunmen, or to surrender, and they had no illusions about their fate if they did that either. They'd be tried, perhaps — if they weren't summarily lynched first — and then they'd be hanged.

Jubal braced into the ferocity of that attack. Bullets struck on both sides and in front of him. He heard the outlaws coming as well as saw their muzzleblasts, bluish and thick from pistols, lance-like and reddish from the Winchester carbines. He flattened, fired, rolled and fired again. When his carbine was shot out he left it and drew his sixgun. Behind him, those possemen suddenly veered away as bullets sang close, and started their charge from a more southerly direction. Down there Ted Withers jumped up to avoid being trampled and loped off towards the east.

The battle suddenly turned; Jubal's charging foemen swung towards the south, where the riders were hauling back as though to dismount and enter the fight on foot, and ran ahead once more. A solitary rider came spurring in from the west. He fired once with a carbine before he could have had a decent target, then let off a wild Comanche howl. For a second this reckless rider distracted everyone, but particularly old Jubal who lay in the path of the running horse. He yelled once for the rider to veer off, when the horseman didn't heed him, Jubal had to spring up and leg it hard off to his left, which was northward.

The possemen called over, identifying themselves. Old Jack Hart also roared out for the gunfire to cease; for the outlaws to surrender. It was a heroic thing to do. Instantly six guns, three forty-five, three carbines, zeroed-in on Marshal Hart. He fell, riddled, and his possemen scattered left and right, which was what the outlaws wanted. They then ran desperately for the possemen's abandoned, bewildered saddle-horses.

The men from Spencer jumped up and ran down towards the southward desert also. They could see those three outlaws, finally, fleeing through the night, but none of them fired. Juan Turcio yelled out a warning, but it wasn't necessary; they'd all seen that solitary mounted figure dip hard to his left and hook his frantic mount into a belly-down run straight at the fleeing men. He rode on a loose-rein, firing his carbine.

When it was empty he hurled it away and went for his forty-five.

The outlaws had to stop and turn back, but the rider was too close. They missed him with their first five shots. He got right up to them, spun across their front and deliberately shot one outlaw three times in the body before his horse gave a tremendous leap into the air, and collapsed, shot dead under the gunman.

Two of the outlaws turned to stagger onward towards the abandoned horses. One of them whirled when a bullet tore away his hat. Long-legged Jeff Pierce was panting from the exertion and was closing in. The outlaw threw down but Jeff fired first. The man stumbled, tried to run on, then fell to one knee. Jeff danced sideways, let the renegade's slug go past, then cut the man down with three thumbed-off shots fired so fast they sounded almost simultaneous. The outlaw dropped forward, tried to brace himself on one arm, but it buckled, dumping him head-on into the churned dust and dirt.

The remaining man reached the horses but they shied away as he lunged left and right. Their bodies, however protected him. The possemen came rushing in now, finally, seeing that one man might escape. Farthest back old Jubal panted along until he came to the dead horse of the lone rider. He looked, slammed to a hard halt and looked closer. It was young Bob pinned under the dead animal by one leg, knocked unconscious. Jubal peered down where the escaping renegade had finally caught an animal. He looked back at his son. Finally, he knelt, bent down to see whether Bob was breathing or not, determined that in fact he was breathing, then Jubal rocked back onto one knee, raised his .45 across the forearm of his raised, motionless left arm, tracked that rising figure as the escaping man heaved himself upright across a horse, and fired.

The outlaw threw up both hands, flung away his gun and fell backwards across the terrified horse's rump. The animal gave a startled bound forward to escape that unaccustomed weight back there and slid from beneath the shot man. The horse bolted straight southward in a flinging run and the man turned once in the air and landed face-down.

Jubal looked around, saw all the others rushing towards those three renegades, put his his empty sixgun and knelt to gently lift young Bob's head, shove his hat under, and to afterwards begin clawing at the soft earth to free his son's broken leg.

Sam Salton came over and helped free young Bob. One of the possemen ran down to the horses and ran back with a canteen of water. Ted Withers and Jeff stood above the man Jeff had killed, breathing hard. It had been a hectic, mad, final ten minutes. The others all came along. Frank Hudson was limping. He'd caught a slug while trying to crawl under one of the freight outfits after freeing the horses. It had been Frank, considering himself done for, whom Ted Withers had heard dully cursing back at the first stage of the fight.

Juan Turcio rounded up the freighters, who were bewildered and hiding in one of the wagons, herded them southward without explaining anything to them, and when another one came unsteadily up with a bloody scalp and lunged at Ted from behind, Juan fired a shot between the man's feet, halting him very effectively.

Ted turned, recognized the freighter who he'd struck over the head, and asked around if anyone had a shot of whiskey. There was liquor up in the wagon-camp. Ted accompanied the man he'd struck up there to help find it.

Jubal called Jeff over. Frank came too. They made young Bob comfortable. Frank said they'd have to send back to town for a wagon; that Bob couldn't be moved until his leg had been splinted. Then Frank also said, easing down gingerly, "I don't feel up to ridin' back either."

Two of the outlaws were alive, but just barely. One was Mike Donlan, the man old Jubal had shot in the back, unseating him as he was on the verge of escaping. The third man was riddled; he'd only had a brief glimpse of Jeff before he'd died. They also carried Marshal Hart back to camp. Two possemen stoked up the little fire. Except for Frank, young Bob, and one or two others with minor injuries, the men from Spencer as well as the townsmen from Daggett were unhurt. Their only real casualty was Marshal Hart, and in his pragmatic way Frank Hudson made a tart observation about that.

"He stood straight up where they couldn't miss him. I'll tell you what I think. I think Marshal Hart's been lookin' for that particular bullet a long time. Tonight he found it."

The pair of shot outlaws were not going to make it. Old Jubal told the one he'd shot this was so. The outlaw, with a broken back and internal injuries, studied Jubal's face a moment before speaking. He didn't seem to be in very much pain, but his tongue was thick, the words dragged, and eventually his eyelids also got very heavy.

"Who — the hell — are you, old man?" he asked.

Jubal answered quietly and bluntly. He told how long he and his sons had been on the trail. He also said it was fortunate the last of the fugitives were going to die; he made no secret at all of the fact that if they didn't die here, he'd stay on their trail until he did kill them.

Sam Salton, standing behind Jubal, eased around. "Donlan; where's the money from the Spencer bank?"

Donlan's lips curled in weak defiance. "Go to hell," he said, and let all his breath out, loosened up and down and closed his eyes. Mike Donlan had also expired.

Juan Turcio came back from the freighter-camp carrying three sets of battered old leather saddlebags slung carelessly over his arms. He arrived just in time to hear Donlan's last words and see Donlan die. He nudged Sam Salton and tossed the saddlebags at his feet.

"Look inside," Turcio said. "They're full of money. It'll be from Spencer and I reckon from a lot of murdered folks we'll never know about. Anyway; there's all they took from your bank and a sight more to boot."

Jeff was with his brother. They were talking. Ted Withers, assuming command after Jack Hart's death, sent several possemen back to Daggett for wagons, and to also catch all the loose horses which had been permitted to escape during the fighting. He then went over where Frank was kneeling beside the last of the wounded outlaws and knelt down.

Frank was explaining in his dull voice who he was and why he was going to hunker right there and rejoice when the injured man died. The outlaw seemed to have trouble focusing his eyes on Frank, but he said, "All right, mister, sit and watch. I can't stop you now anyway. An' I hope it makes you feel good. But I got somethin' to tell you — I didn't join Donlan until the week after they'd done that down in Deaf Smith County. I joined 'em when they was headin' back over into New Mexico out of Texas."

Frank said nothing. He sat and traded looks with the dying man. Finally, still as expressionless and dull-eyed as before, Frank twisted up a cigarette, lit it, and wordlessly shoved it between the dying man's lips. The outlaw smiled with only his loosening lips, tried to inhale, didn't make it, and closed his eyes. Ted Withers lightly tapped Frank, got up and walked away.

It was all finished. What those Texans had spent nearly two sleepless, haunted months bringing to an end, was finished. Out of all those killers only one was still alive, Pat Potter. He would die on the gallows; that was a foregone conclusion too. But Ted Withers made a private wager with himself; he bet the men from Deaf Smith County would linger in New Mexico Territory long enough to witness that hanging.

He was right. Dead right.

180